*The
Great
Rope*

Rosemary S. Nesbitt
The Great Rope

☆ ☆ ☆ ☆ ☆

ILLUSTRATED BY DOUGLAS GORSLINE

Lothrop, Lee & Shepard Co., Inc.
NEW YORK

For *George*,
with whom it all began,
and for
Mary, *Annie*, *Corky*,
and
Betsy—a legacy

Contents

Foreword

UP IN THE NORTH COUNTRY there is a great blue lake. New York State makes a sickle bend around its southern shore and Canada fills out the long curve on the other side. About halfway along the "York State" side, a deep, green river cuts the shore and joins the Great Lakes water route to the heartland of the northeast. In ancient times, the Iroquois called this place "Ochoueguen," which means "The Flowing Out of the Waters." They called their great blue lake "Skanadario." After the white man came, the softly musical Indian names passed through harsher tongues: French, German, Dutch, English. The lake became "Ontario," and "Ochoueguen" was distorted until it was finally called "Oswego." The coming of the white man brought harsher times, too. For over two hundred years after the discovery of America, men were continually fighting for control of the forts at Oswego and the river which they protected. This book deals with the story of one of those battles.

It is a true story. I wrote it because I wanted my children to know about the boy, Jonathan, who was their great-great-grandfather. Jonathan's story takes place during the War of 1812. Some people refer to this conflict as the "Forgotten War." This is true partly because so many of its events happened in remote, widely separated places. And also because there were no war correspondents to record what happened, only the participants, who were usually content to pass on what they had seen by word of mouth. Nevertheless, there were many brave and heroic men who contributed to the story of America during that war. Andrew Jackson, Stephen Decatur, and Oliver Hazard Perry were among them. So were Jonathan Cooper, Melancthon T. Woolsey, George Mitchell, and Isaac Chauncey. We don't know everything that Jonathan said and did, but the battles he saw, the places he went, and the people he met are all part of Oswego's history. They are part of American history too, and so is the story of the great rope.

If you come to northern York State today, you can visit many of the places and see many of the things mentioned in the story. Fort Ontario and Sackets Harbor are still here; you can drive over the route of the great rope; and Onundiaga's people still live, right where they always did, just south of Salt Point, or Syracuse, as it is now called. Jonathan's great-great-grandchildren are here too, and we live on a site only a little way from where the log house stood.

We all hope you will come.

Rosemary S. Nesbitt

☆ **I**

Where Are They?

JONATHAN COOPER came up to the log house, piled the wood he had been carrying neatly beside the front door, and turned to look back. It was just before first dark, and he knew that when they finally came, this would not be the time. Still, it was good to make certain.

The Cooper house stood on the high ground at the top of Aries Street. Jonathan, standing on the doorstep, looked carefully down over the village, then out to the harbor, and finally back to the bright line of the river and the wharves, empty now, save for the little gunboat "Growler" and the schooner "Syren," which rocked gently in their slips. Joel Tyler was tying the ferry and securing it for the night at the foot of Aries Street. The long rays of the sun etched the lake in clear relief.

There was nothing there. The curfew gun at the fort barked sharply. Night was beginning. They had not come.

Jonathan was surprised to discover that he had been holding his breath. Now he let it out in a long sigh, and sat down on the step to scrape the mud from his shoes. Where were they? Where were the British? It was the fourth of May, 1814, and the war had been going on for two years now. Almost a year ago, in June, they had attacked Fort Ontario and tried to take Oswego. They had been beaten off that time. But they would be back. The British didn't give up so easily. Jonathan's grandfather had said so and he ought to know. He had marched against them with Nicholas Herkimer and Marinus Willett.

Jonathan was worried and getting more worried every day. Not about himself. He knew he could take care of himself. And not about his mother or his father. His father was the captain of the militia and he was sure to know what to do when the time came. And his mother had been born on the frontier. She was just like his grandfather—tough, brave, and stubborn. She had refused, point blank, to go out east to Scriba where his grandfather lived. She would have been safe there. Most of the other women and children had left the village long ago, when the war had first started and there had been talk that the British might arouse the Indians as they had during the War of the Revolution. But his mother hadn't left—not Alice Cooper.

No, it wasn't his parents he was worried about, it was the great rope. It was the last thing he thought about at night and the first thing in the morning. The British must not get the great rope. They must not!

Jonathan lifted the heavy latch and stepped into the big square room that was his home. The sight of the room always pleased him, but never more than during these days since the emergency had begun. The great four-poster bed in the corner, the hutch cupboard on the opposite wall with its neat rows of blue china, the tall square desk in the corner with the old-fashioned silver inkwell and the two white quills, the hand-sewn orange and black rag rug on the floor; it was all there. Everything was in its place.

His mother was kneading bread at the long sawbuck table. When she heard Jonathan, she turned and smiled at him. She had on a fresh apron and her thick, brown braids, shining and newly brushed, lay in a coronet across the top of her head. She stood tall and moved quickly as she always did, but her blue eyes were shadowed and Jonathan knew she had spent another uncertain day, watching and waiting. She set three bowls of hot venison stew on the table and poured three mugs of cool, thick buttermilk.

"They did not come again today," he said.

"No, Jonathan, they did not come." The relief in her voice was almost like a prayer.

"That means the rope is still safe."

"You musn't worry so about the rope. Your father and the rest of the men will keep that safe, no matter what happens."

Jonathan was about to say he was sure that was so, when the low murmur of men's voices came filtering through the half-open window. His mother moved swiftly across the room and put a trencher of bread on the table. Jonathan ran to the door to meet his father.

James Cooper seemed to fill the doorway—and then the room. It wasn't just his size, although he was a big man, well over six feet and heavy set. It was his presence. His Scots ancestors had left him their reserve and their thick shocks of prematurely gray hair. They had also left him their gentleness, their firmness, and their courage. He came in now, kissed Jonathan's mother, and stood his long rifle in the corner, just beside the door. Then, slowly and deliberately as he did everything, he took the powder horn from around his neck and shoulder and carefully looped it over the barrel of the gun. Jonathan couldn't remember how long it had been since his father had hung the gun on the two pegs which had been placed over the fireplace to hold it. It seemed a long time, too, since he had gone to work without the rifle on his shoulder. James Cooper turned and touched Jonathan's hair. Then he moved back to the doorway.

"Come in, gentlemen."

Mr. Alvin Bronson and Mr. Matthew McNair followed Jonathan's father into the house. Jonathan started a little when he saw them; they looked so out of place here. Mr. Bronson—short, stocky, his black beard circling his round firm chin like a wreath; and Mr. McNair—tall, thin as a Kentucky rifle, and clean-shaven, with a great, high-bridged nose and a wiry thatch of flaming red hair. Jonathan thought Mr. McNair looked a lot like a picture he'd seen of General Andrew Jackson.

It was a fine thing, Jonathan thought, the way these two important men came to his father for his opinion. Of course, James Cooper had been a captain in the militia for two years and he was the best navigator on the Great Lakes; still, Mr. Bronson and Mr. McNair were the most important men in Oswego.

Alvin Bronson owned a big warehouse and forwarding business, and he had been made military storekeeper for the district by President Madison himself. Mr. McNair had a forwarding business too, but he was also a shipbuilder. James Cooper worked for him and had been foreman during the construction of the fifty-ton schooner "Linda." When the war started, the government had armed the "Linda" and all of the other Oswego ships. They were all out on the lake, now, patrolling against the British.

Mr. McNair had been given the post of commissioner of subsistence. Jonathan wasn't quite sure what that meant, but he knew it was important. But it was

James Cooper who knew the lakes. He knew the currents and the bays and the coves. When the British finally came, he would be most likely to know when and how they would do it.

All of these thoughts raced through Jonathan's mind as he watched the two men come into the log house. They always smiled when they saw Jonathan and quite often Mr. McNair had a piece of hard taffy or a ball of resin gum in his pocket. But this evening things were not the same. The two men spoke pleasantly to Jonathan and his mother, but they seemed to be thinking about something else and they did not smile. They refused Alice Cooper's offer of supper, but did sit down, pulling their chairs close to the table. Mr. Bronson reached into his right-hand weskit pocket and took out a pair of round, steel-rimmed spectacles. He placed them firmly on his nose and fitted the rounded ends carefully over his ears. Then he cleared his throat and spoke.

"A runner came in from Sackets a few minutes ago, James. He brought a message from Chauncey." Mr. Bronson's voice was low and even.

"Will you read it now, or would you like Alice and Jonathan to step outside?" James Cooper asked.

"No, there is no reason why they shouldn't hear this."

"Then get on with it, Alvin." Mr. McNair's impatience showed in every angle of his long body.

Mr. Bronson carefully unfolded a thin strip of foolscap and began to read.

1 May, 1814

Honorable Alvin Bronson, Esquire
Port of Oswego
State of New York

Dear Sir:

I beg leave to inform you that on the morning of this day, May 1, 1814, we have launched the frigate "Superior." The gunboats "Mohawk" and "Jones," which are nearing completion, are still in the stocks. I know I do not need to impress upon you the importance of getting these ships out on the lake as soon as possible. Our little fleet from last year which is in port here numbers only sixteen vessels and the largest of these mounts only 34 guns. However, when she is armed, the "Superior" will mount 66 guns, and the "Mohawk" and the "Jones," although smaller, will mount 70 guns between them. Then we can go out and meet the British on their own terms. The enemy knows this. They also know that the rigging, armament, and other supplies for our three new ships is in Oswego on its way here. They will try to prevent the supplies from reaching us, for to do this would be equivalent to the destruction of our squadron, as without them the new ships could not appear on the lake, nor could our other fleet venture out in the presence of the greatly increased naval armament of the enemy, with the slightest hope of success. I urge you, Mr. Bronson, and the patriotic citizens of Oswego, to do all in your power to prevent our supplies from falling into enemy hands. Prepare well for the attack on your port which is bound to come soon. I regret that we have no additional troops to send you and pray that all may go well with your heroic endeavor.

Your obedient servant,

Isaac Chauncey
Commodore Commanding
United States Fleet
Sackets Harbor

It was very quiet in the room. Jonathan could hear a log snap in the fireplace and the soft scraping of the crickets outside the door. It was Mr. McNair who finally broke the silence.

"Tell us what you think, James." There was urgency and respect in his voice.

James Cooper got up and walked slowly over to the mantel. He took his old-fashioned, long-stemmed clay pipe from its rack, filled it, and then lit it from a brand which he took from the fireplace.

"I think we had better post double watches during the early morning from now on," he said.

"Then you think the attack will come soon?"

"The winds and the currents are all favorable right now."

"Then they're as good as here." Mr. McNair's voice had such a finality about it that suddenly Jonathan felt a lump in his throat.

Mr. Bronson got up and walked over to the window. "Well, we've always known it had to come. After all, this is the richest prize in the north. Whoever controls Lake Ontario and the mouth of the Oswego River controls the entire northeast. The British have to get it if they want to win."

Jonathan couldn't remember how many times he had heard Mr. Bronson say this; and every time it seemed to Jonathan that he left out the most important thing of all.

"They want the great rope too, don't they, Mr. Bronson?" Jonathan felt his face starting to burn; he hadn't meant to say it out loud. The men all turned and looked at him.

"Yes, Jonathan, you're quite right. They want the rope." Mr. Bronson's tone was serious and grave. Mr. McNair looked up and said sharply, "You still fussing about that rope, boy?"

Jonathan found himself tongue-tied with embarrassment and his father answered for him. "Ever since we moved all the stores into the woods and up river to the Falls for safekeeping, Jonathan has been worried about the great rope for the 'Superior.' "

Mr. McNair got up and walked over to stand beside Jonathan. "Yes, I know he has," he said. "He told me all about it when you brought him down to the yard one day. Seemed to me, anybody that interested ought to know all the facts, so I told him a few things about the great rope, as he calls it, and the rest of the rigging. Let's see how much you remember, boy."

Jonathan's mouth felt as dry as parchment. Desperately he looked around the room; first to his father and then to his mother. "Go ahead, Jonathan." His father nodded and motioned with his pipe. His mother reached over and gently patted his arm. But it was Mr. Bronson who, in his quiet way, put Jonathan at ease.

"Please do go ahead, Jonathan," he said politely. "I'd like to hear about the great rope. You know, I've been so busy lately, I think I may have forgotten some of the things you're going to say."

Jonathan looked gratefully at Mr. Bronson, got to his feet, and in one breath blurted out the story.

"The great rope is the main anchor cable for the 'Superior.' It is twenty-two inches around and it weighs nine thousand, six hundred pounds. And it's the thing Commodore Chauncey needs most because everybody knows you can't take a sailing vessel out without an anchor."

For the first time that evening everybody, even Jonathan's mother, smiled. Mr. McNair was smiling too, but his tone was still sharp. "Well go on boy, finish it. Why can't you take a sailing vessel out without an anchor?"

Jonathan took another deep breath and went on.

"Because a sailing vessel can't stop and hold its position without an anchor. That means that Commodore Chauncey couldn't blockade a port or stop to fire on an enemy fort or even come back home and stay in port without an anchor. I know the other cables and the guns and food are important—Commodore Chauncey needs them all. But it's the great rope he's *got* to have and we can't let the British get it. We just can't!"

Everybody stopped smiling then, and it was very quiet in the room. They all looked at Jonathan for a minute and then his father said, "You're quite right, Jonathan. We can't."

Then he turned to Alvin Bronson and Matthew Mc-Nair. "Chauncey's letter states the whole case very clearly. If he doesn't get those supplies he can't move out of Sackets Harbor. Sir James Yeo knows that and that's why he's bringing such a big fleet in here to attack us. He wants those stores! If he gets them, we can forget about Lake Ontario, and the Oswego River and everything else. We'll all be citizens of the Crown again. So, we not only have to see that Yeo doesn't get your rope, Jonathan, we have to figure out a way of getting it past him and up to Commodore Chauncey at Sackets Harbor."

Mr. Bronson looked at Jonathan's father. Then he said, steadily but in a very low voice, "But James, that's why the navy left the 'Growler' here in the harbor and that's why I kept the 'Syren' in my slip. We're

waiting for a chance to put the stores aboard and try for a run past the British."

Again the room was very quiet. Jonathan counted ten ticks from the steeple clock on the mantel before his father answered. "That, sir, is what I meant to suggest. I think the time for using the 'Growler' and the 'Syren' is past. We'll have to think of some other way."

Mr. McNair cleared his throat and said, "What you say makes sense, James. We'll have to try something else. Confound it! We've got to do something about Chauncey and we've got to do it fast. He got that frigate built in eighty days and now he's got to sit up there at Sackets until we figure out a way to get his supplies to him."

Mr. Bronson got to his feet, bowed to Jonathan's mother, and picking up his tall beaver hat, said, "Thank you, James. You've told us what we came to hear."

Mr. McNair cleared his throat again. "Yes, James, you've a good head and a solid point of view. Thank you. Get your supper now, and a bit of rest before you come out on the watch. Good evening, Mrs. Cooper. Young man, you're a good Scotsman, and you know, they make the best Americans!"

Jonathan was speechless. He knew that this was the highest compliment a McNair from Ayrshire, Scotland, could give.

☆ **2**

Suppose
There Is
Fire?

AFTER MR. BRONSON and Mr. McNair had left, Jonathan and his mother and father sat down at the table. They didn't talk very much and when they had finished eating, James Cooper got up and walked over to the peg beside the hutch cupboard where his uniform coat was hanging.

Jonathan watched solemnly as his father shrugged the blue coat with the buff facings over his big shoulders. He had always been very proud to have Captain James Cooper for his father; there was nothing he liked better than to follow him down to the muster. But for the last month there had been no muster; every night James Cooper had been standing in with his men on the night watch. There weren't enough soldiers at Oswego to guard the fort and the harbor, too.

Jonathan's mother was busy stuffing half a loaf of bread and some dried venison into his father's pouch, but she was looking at her husband all the time. Now she said, "Where will you be tonight?"

"Down on the west bluff, above the old reservation."

"Be careful, James."

His father didn't answer. Instead he turned and put both arms around his wife and kissed her, hard. Jonathan looked on in astonishment. It was very unusual for his parents to behave so.

"Jonathan." His father's voice was firm. "I know I can depend on you to do exactly as your mother says."

Jonathan nodded. For some reason he couldn't seem to find anything to say. Then his father smiled, exchanged another quick look with his mother, and was gone. Alice Cooper stood in the door for a moment looking after him; then she closed it and turned back into the room.

"Jonathan, I want you to get the lantern and collect all of the buckets we have, all except the household bucket; and you'd better look for the big gourds too. Take them out to the well and fill them. Then bring them back here and line them up outside, right next to the door."

Startled, Jonathan said, "Why, Mother?"

His mother hesitated for a minute and then she said, "The attack will be soon now, son. We must be prepared for fire."

"Fire!" Jonathan had not thought about that. "Will the British burn our house?"

"Not the British themselves, but if there are Indians with them, we can't be sure."

"But Onundiaga said that all of the Indians had agreed to be on our side. He heard Red Jacket say it himself, at the conference, in Buffalo."

"I know, Jonathan, but Red Jacket speaks only for the Six Nations of the Iroquois. We don't know about the Shawnees and the Delawares and the Wyandottes."

"But Onundiaga said—"

"Onundiaga doesn't want to worry us. Now hurry and get the water."

Jonathan had always admired and respected his mother very much; but never more than now. She was so calm and her voice was so firm. He had a feeling that the Indians would not burn this house. Nevertheless, Jonathan took up the lantern and went out through the shed. He decided he would speak to Onundiaga about the Shawnees and the other Indians the next time Onundiaga came down from Salt Point. Jonathan and all the other boys in the village thought Onundiaga was the most unusual Indian in the country. He kept a wickiup in the village of his tribe, the Onondagas, but he spent most of his time on the trail between Oswego and Salt Point carrying the mail.

Nobody could recall how Onundiaga had come to be the mail carrier, but for as long as Jonathan could remember, Onundiaga had come trotting down the trail every Thursday at four o'clock with the fat buckskin pouch slung over his shoulder. He no longer wore paint of any kind but he had kept his bristling, black scalp-lock with the two heron feathers trailing down the back. He wore buckskin breeches and a shirt with yellow porcupine quills running down the sleeves. Onundiaga scorned all jewelry except for the silver gorget around his neck which his father had received from George Washington after the war. Jonathan thought he was the most beautifully dressed man he had ever seen —especially here in Oswego where all the men and boys, except for Mr. Bronson and Mr. McNair, dressed alike. It was like a uniform; they all wore sheep's-gray pants and weskits because it was the only yarn the women had.

Jonathan would never say anything to his mother, but he was very tired of it. One day he had asked Onundiaga for a shirt and moccasins like his. Onundiaga answered by saying that Indian boys didn't get that kind of shirt and moccasins until they could prove they were men. When Jonathan had asked him what he had to do to prove his manhood, Onundiaga had said, "When the time comes, you will know." Jonathan knew he had to be content with that, but he thought about it again as he walked around the shed looking for the gourds. He wondered if he would ever do anything important enough to earn one of those beautiful shirts.

He found six buckets and four large gourds. They

were heavy when they were full, but Jonathan managed to get them around to the front door without spilling very much of the water. After that he went inside and, closing the door for the night, slipped the big bar firmly into its stanchions. His mother was just finishing the supper dishes. Jonathan banked the fire and snuffed out the candles on the mantelpiece. Then, as he had done every night since his father had been standing guard, he helped his mother turn the big bed down for the night.

The first thing they did was to unfold the blue and white quilt. Jonathan looked, as he always did, for the corner where the writing was. It said, *"James and Alice, 14 October, 1800."* His mother had made it; it was her wedding quilt. Jonathan thought it was very beautiful and besides that, it was like a history book. It marked the beginning of their family. His mother and father had been married in the first year of the new century, and two years later he had been born. He was only twelve, but his family was as old as the century. Jonathan thought that made everything seem solid and permanent. He tucked the quilt in firmly around the foot of the feather tick and then turned to the hutch cupboard for his bed candle.

"Is there anything else you need, Mother?"

His mother took up her candle and came toward him across the room. The soft light shone upward against her face, smoothing away the lines of work and worry.

She touched the tip of her candle to his, very gently. "No thank you, Jonathan. Good night."

They stood for a moment looking at each other; then Jonathan went over and began to climb the ladder into the loft. Just before he reached the top he turned and looked back. His mother was standing where he had left her, watching him.

"You may keep your candle and read for a while, if you like."

Jonathan was delighted. There had been so little time for reading lately. He nodded and hurried on up the ladder. As he got to the top he paused, with just his head and shoulders clearing the floor level. Jonathan loved the loft room; it was his special place and not just because he slept there. It was where he kept his most precious things. It was where he came when he wanted to think about something or when he wanted to read. He let his eyes move slowly over the room.

At one end was the little gable window. His father had cut it into the north wall after his mother had said that Jonathan would suffocate on hot summer nights without any air up there. To the right of the window was his bed, tucked tightly under the eaves. Jonathan couldn't imagine a better place for a bed. The roof sloped right down over his head, and it seemed to him that even through the thickness of board and shingle he could put up his hand and feel the wind or the rain or even the quiet—whatever the night might bring—closing over him like a blessing.

Running straight across the ceiling was the rooftree
—a huge beam which his father had smoothed with an
adze. From the beam hung the sweet herbs: camomile
and rhubarb and lavender. Jonathan liked the lavender
best; it reminded him of his mother. Alongside the
herbs hung four dried haunches of venison which his
father had bought for twenty-five cents from two
Oneidas. His father had precious little time for hunting
these days. Or fishing either. Next to the venison Jonathan had hung the long strings of dried salmon. He
never looked at them without remembering; two hundred and forty salmon caught in four hours' time, and
half of them were his. The river that day had looked
alive, so tightly were the fish packed together as they
swam upstream to spawn. Maybe next year there
would be time to fish again.

There was one more thing in the loft; something
Jonathan had made and put there himself. It was his
shelf. He had fitted it into the wall right over the head
of his bed so that he could reach it, even at night. On
the shelf were the things Jonathan valued most in the
world. There was a little one-pound round shot he had
picked up over near the fort. It had fallen there during
the battle a year ago. Next to that was half an egg shell;
but this was no ordinary egg shell—it was a goose egg
and it had shaped the most delicious maple candy Jonathan had ever tasted. He had gotten that last year too,
when they had gone to the spring sugaring-off at his
grandfather's farm. And then there were his books.

There weren't very many books in Oswego in 1814, and Jonathan had more than any other boy. This was because his father had been a ship's carpenter, not just on the Great Lakes, but out on the ocean as well. And these had been the books he had taken with him, in his sea chest, to teach himself navigation. He had given the books to Jonathan, reminding him how rare and valuable they were. Jonathan had read them all: *The New Practical Navigator*, *The Ship Builder's Assistant*, and the one he liked best, *A Sailor's Peregrinations on the Seven Seas*. Jonathan didn't understand everything that was in them yet. But someday he would, and in the meantime he liked them much better than some of the books Dr. Caldwell brought to the school.

Thoughtfully he looked at his things. Suppose in the battle the house *should* catch fire. He could always get another egg shell and the cannon ball would not burn, but what about the books? If these were destroyed, they could never be replaced. Then he remembered the canvas. He had an old piece of canvas under his bed that Mr. McNair had given him for running errands down at the shipyard. Quickly he pulled it out and wrapped it around his books. Then he sat down on the edge of his bed and waited.

In a few minutes the soft light filtering up between the floor boards went out. Jonathan sat quietly for what seemed to him a very long time. Then, gathering his bundle tightly in one arm, he slid down the ladder. His mother's breathing was gentle and regular. He tiptoed past the bed and over to the door. Jonathan was tall and strong for his age, but he had to strain every muscle in his arms and back in order to get the bar off the door without making any noise. Then he slipped out into the yard.

The moon had risen; it was full, and Jonathan was grateful for that. He wouldn't have dared risk a lantern; that would be just like a beacon for the British. There was a little chokecherry tree in the corner of the yard, and it was here that Jonathan buried his books. He decided not to tell his mother. It might upset her if she thought he was really afraid that their house might be burned.

And inside, Alice Cooper lay back upon the goose-down pillows. She would never tell Jonathan that she had seen him, but tomorrow she would tell James. There were precious few boys on the frontier who knew the value of a book. James had done his work well.

His mother's position had not changed when Jonathan slipped back into the house. He ran quietly up the ladder, undressed, and stretched out on the soft tick. I will rest a minute, he thought, and then I will keep watch.

He was dreaming about it a few minutes later when his mother pulled the patchwork quilt over him and softly blew out the candle.

☆ 3

The British Are Here!

JONATHAN WOKE UP SUDDENLY and then lay very quiet, listening. It was just before first light. If they were coming today, this would be the time. The gray light of predawn sifted through the gable window like Indian smoke. All of Jonathan's world lay perfectly still. Then the great, green frog in the pond down the road began his rhythmical, throaty salute to the day. The pigeons who lived in the cote on top of the shed answered him. Finally Jonathan heard the squeak and creak of the rope springs on the big bed down below. That meant his mother was stirring and would soon be up, waiting for his father.

Jonathan rolled out of bed and padded to the window, half crouching under the low gable of the roof. He paused for a moment before looking out; would they be here this morning? He ducked his head and peered through the little, uneven squares of bottle glass. The world had disappeared.

An early spring fog, not uncommon on the lakes, had covered everything like a huge, gray eiderdown. Jonathan could barely make out the handle of the well sweep which was only thirty feet from the door. He shivered; the room was damp and chill. He hurried over and stood near the chimney to dress; the stones were still warm from last night's fire. He had barely placed his foot on the first rung of the ladder when the warm, golden glow of the fat table candle floated up around him. Alice Cooper was standing by the fireplace, reddening the breakfast coals with the small leather bellows.

Jonathan walked over and took the bellows from her, bending to the hearth to continue the work. He cleared his throat and said, "Do you think they're out there in the fog?"

"They may be. But I do not think it is likely. We would have heard something."

Jonathan set the bellows in its rack beside the fireplace; then he took the household bucket from its peg over the table.

"I'll get the water. Father will probably be late this

morning. They won't leave the watch until the fog lifts."

"That's right." His mother's voice was steady but she did not look around. "Be careful, Jonathan, don't . . ." She paused a moment. "Don't fall."

"I won't, Mother. I'll be right back." Jonathan stepped out into the damp, gray morning. The wind from the southeast had freshened and now he could see across the river, clear over to the fort. The fog had rolled down in front of the wind until now it was hanging just inside the harbor. At the foot of the street, he could just make out stocky little Joel Tyler getting ready to untie the ferry.

Joel was only nine, but since his father had gone out on the lake in command of the schooner "Eagle," Joel had been left in charge of the ferry. At any other time he would have been the envy of every boy in the district, but now they were all doing men's work. Dr. Caldwell, who also served as schoolmaster, had understood the wisdom of this and had closed the school. Carlos Colton, who was Jonathan's best friend, was working every day now for Mr. Bronson.

Jonathan himself had been working for his father and as a runner for the militia. He knew so much about boats and could row so well that he had been kept busy taking materials and supplies back and forth from the village to the fort. In Jonathan's mind, however, the most important thing he had done was to help build "Tent City." Thinking about that now, he turned and walked to the corner of the house where he stopped and looked to the south. The shore line sloped upward on both sides of the river. The village had been built on the west side, on the flats, and part way up the slope. The Cooper house was the last one at the end of Aries Street. To the south of it, between Taurus and Gemini Streets, there was a broad meadow which extended for almost half a mile before the hill continued. And now, covering the meadow in a sea of canvas, stood Tent City.

Colonel Mitchell, who was in command at Fort Ontario, was a clever soldier and a determined one. He knew he was going to be greatly outnumbered by the British, but he had made up his mind that he was not going to be outsmarted by them. So he had recruited every man and boy in the village and set them to work building a false military encampment in the meadow beside the Cooper house. Jonathan had helped and he thought it was a great joke on the British.

They had collected every piece of canvas, every tarpaulin, every old sail, everything that looked the least bit like tent material. Then they had built a city of tents in the meadow. Of course nobody lived in them. But the British didn't know that and Colonel Mitchell hoped they wouldn't get close enough to find out. He hoped they'd be fooled into thinking he had three times the men who were actually on duty at Fort Ontario. Jonathan hoped so too. He had great faith in Colonel Mitchell and thought he was much smarter than any British officer was likely to be. Jonathan was glad Colonel Mitchell had been sent to Oswego. He acted as though there were no such word as defeat.

They had worked so hard to build Oswego—his father and Mr. Bronson and Mr. McNair and all the others. The village had been growing steadily before the war; there were about thirty houses now. A little more than half of them were built of logs like Jonathan's, but the others were frame buildings and some of them even had two stories. The houses were scattered over a dozen streets, neatly divided into blocks. The streets running north and south were called First, Second, Third, and Fourth; but those going east and west had wonderful names. They were called Aries and Taurus; Sagittarius and Gemini; Aquila, Lyra, and Capricornus. Jonathan knew them all by heart and he knew what they meant, too. They were names of the constellations, and they were all in his navigation books. He remembered how surprised Dr. Caldwell and the class had been when he got to his feet one day and told them all about it.

It seemed to Jonathan that the village was very complete. There weren't any churches yet, which was the only thing his mother didn't like. But there were four stores, the school, three taverns, and, of course, the

Bronson and McNair warehouses. And every now and then a traveling minister came through and conducted services in the school. The thing Jonathan liked best about that was the horn the minister blew to let everybody know when the service was going to begin.

It all looked just the same as Jonathan stood looking down, except for one thing. The ships were missing. Before the war, the harbor had looked like a forest, there were so many tall-masted schooners and brigs riding in the slips. Now, except for the "Growler" and the "Syren," they were all gone. Jonathan missed them, especially the "Oneida" and her lusty, powerful crew. These men laughed a great deal and their singing filled the air from reveille to retreat. Looking toward the fog-shrouded slip where the "Oneida" had been berthed, it seemed to Jonathan that he could still hear the final verse of the crew's favorite work chanty:

> It oft times has been told,
> That the British seamen bold,
> Could flog the tars of France
>   so neat and handy—o;
> But they never found their match,
> Till the Yankees them did catch,
> O the Yankee boys for fighting
>   are the dandy—o!

Jonathan drew the water and took the bucket in. Alice Cooper watched her sturdy, serious son as he carefully poured some of it into the kettle and then swung it in over the fire to heat. He had her deep blue eyes and soft, straight, brown hair, but he had his father's long bones and his broad, square shoulders. He had James's way, too, she thought; considerate, deliberate, and gentle. Now he seemed old before it was time. It wasn't just that he was tall for his twelve years; Jonathan understood the terrible time they were going through. She had hoped he wouldn't have to know about such things so soon. She wanted to tell him how proud she was of him; how pleased she was with his gentle, manly way. Instead she said, in what she hoped was a matter-of-fact voice, "Jonathan, will you go up in the loft and see if there is any of your smoked salmon left? I think your father might like it for breakfast."

Jonathan was always pleased when his mother mentioned the salmon. He climbed up the ladder and went to the end of the beam where the fish were hanging. He untied two and was turning to start down when the sun came through the window, sharp and bright as a hunter's knife. From where he stood, Jonathan could see straight down the river and out into the harbor. The fog was sliding away, like a great gray curtain. It was still thick and heavy down near the water, but higher up it was swirling and tearing into long, thin shreds. Pricking through it like a forest in a snowstorm were the mast tips, each one lapped by a square of red bunting, the Maltese cross in blue and white, sharply etched across its field. The great ships of the line seemed to materialize as if they were being conjured up out of the fog.

The British were there.

☆ 4

The
Battle
Begins

ALICE COOPER, bending to take the heated washing water from the fireplace crane, felt the warm sun on her back. "The fog has lifted," she said aloud, and turning, went quickly to the door. She saw them at the instant that Jonathan came sliding down the ladder from the loft.

"Mother, they are here." He was surprised to find himself whispering.

"Yes, Jonathan, they are here."

She slipped her arm around the boy's shoulder and together they stood in the doorway of the log house and watched the British come into their world. The morning was clear now; the wind had shifted to the northeast and taken the fog before it to the west. The sky was blue with great white clouds moving like a reflection of the tall ships below. Jonathan counted eight men-of-war, five gunboats, and about twenty smaller craft; it was difficult to tell how many, since they were partly hidden among the great ships of the line. It looked like a picture, Jonathan thought; one of the pictures he had seen in his navigation books.

For a moment everything was still and then, as if somebody had given a signal, everything started to happen at once. Across the river at the fort, they could see soldiers erupting from every side, taking positions on the ramparts. At the same time a line of horsemen came charging out of the sally port and scattered in all directions.

"Where are they going?" Jonathan's voice was shaking. They couldn't be running away. His mother knew at once what he was thinking.

"Don't you remember your father telling us that the minute the British appeared, Colonel Mitchell was going to send men out into the countryside after the rest of the militia?"

Jonathan took a deep breath; he *had* forgotten. During the past weeks he had come to think of all the militia as being right here in Oswego under his father's command. Feeling his relief, his mother went on. "They will start coming in now, from all over."

"Even from as far as Salt Point and Onondaga Hill?"

"Just as soon as the word gets up river."

Could they get here in time to do any good? Alice Cooper wondered if James would have time to come up and tell them what his plan was, now that they knew the size of the attacking force. The village at their feet had come to life and was bustling with activity; people were running back and forth, putting animals into pens and sheds; closing the heavy shutters over their windows and filling fire pails. But there was no shouting, no screaming, no panic. Alice Cooper felt very proud of her neighbors. So did Jonathan; they'd show the British!

Jonathan had taken care of all the chores the night before, except for closing the shutters. When he started to close them his mother stopped him. She wanted to be able to see James and she wanted to know what the British were going to do. There were two advantages to being the last house up on the high ground. You could see everything that was going on and the range was pretty far.

The last of the horsemen were just disappearing down the military road when a soldier came running out of the fort and over to the west bluff. He ran down the footpath which angled from the fort level to the shore line below. They could see him running up the gangplank of the "Growler" and then he disappeared below decks.

Jonathan's mother turned and hurried into the house; she was back in a minute bringing with her Grandfather Gordon's glass. A spyglass was a precious thing on the frontier and not many people had one. Grandfather Gordon's glass had a fine brass case and it was marked "Edinburgh" on the side. Jonathan had often looked at it but he had never been allowed to touch it. Now he watched his mother put her eye to the eyepiece and adjust the focus.

"They're all leaving the ship," she said, and handed the glass to Jonathan. Too astonished to say anything, he raised the telescope and focused on the "Growler." The soldier had reappeared on deck followed by the crew and their commander, Lieutenant Pearce. The men lined up and Jonathan could see Lieutenant Pearce telling them something. Then, still in the line, they turned, and moving quickly, left the ship and started up the path to the fort. The Lieutenant was the last to leave. Just as he reached the side, he bent over for a moment; then running as fast as he could, he raced down the plank and up the path after the men. Jonathan passed the glass to his mother.

"What are they doing?"

But before she could answer, there was a flash of orange flame, a great burst of black smoke, and a tremendous roar. As the smoke drifted away, Jonathan could see the "Growler" begin to settle slowly into the water.

"They're sinking her! They're sinking the 'Growl-

er'!" His voice shook and his face was white with disbelief.

"They must." His mother's hand on his shoulder was firm. "The British must not be allowed to take her."

"Then father was right." Jonathan swallowed hard. "We'll have to think of another way to get the great rope to Commodore Chauncey."

"We will. We'll find a way." She hoped her voice carried a conviction she did not feel.

Jonathan took up the glass and looked again at the scene in the harbor. The enemy had moved to within a quarter mile of the shore. Now they hove to and started to make preparations to land.

"Mother, look!" Jonathan handed her the glass. "They're not going to shell the fort. They're getting ready to land."

Alice Cooper's heart started to pound and her hands were wet as she lifted the glass. A land engagement! That meant that James would be in the thick of it. She trained the glass on the fort. The village militia were marching in. There were so few of them; she could see James's tall, sturdy figure striding along at the head of the column. Just before he disappeared inside the walls, he turned and looked in the direction of the house; and then he raised his hand. Had the sunlight reflected for an instant from the lens of the glass or had he just known she would be watching? No matter; she felt warmed and comforted by James's salute. There never had been need for many words between them. She turned and handed the glass to Jonathan. They passed it back and forth as they watched the battle begin.

The militia disappeared inside the fort and took up assigned positions. In the meantime, Colonel Mitchell sent an old twelve-pounder, the biggest gun he had, down the bluff with a squad under Captain Boyle and Lieutenant Legate. Jonathan and his mother watched while the men slid the gun down the sheer drop, using only ropes and one old cannon sling. They set it up on the shore a little to the west of the fort. Now the heavy guns on the British men-of-war began a bombardment.

Under the protection of the cannonade, fifteen boats filled with troops began to row rapidly toward the shore. Colonel Mitchell and his men started to return the fire from the warships as vigorously as they could, with the few guns they had. Jonathan turned the glass on Captain Boyle and the twelve-pounder. Under his breath he began to give instructions to the gun crew. "Steady, steady, hold your fire, not yet, not yet, NOW!" There was a tremendous blast from the old gun, right into the midst of the approaching boats. Men, pieces of wood, and weapons went flying into the air and began dropping into the water all mixed up together. The old gun roared again, and again the effect was disastrous for the British.

The smoke was so heavy in the windless spring air that at times the glass was almost useless. Finally, after a third volley, Jonathan could see that three of the boats were completely disabled. What was left of their crews were swimming and bobbing in the water. Two of the other British boats moved out of the formation and began picking up the men from the water. Then, almost as if it had been saving itself for this moment, the old gun thundered again. The flotilla appeared to pause for a moment and sit suspended in the water. Then it swung around and started back toward the mother ships.

Without the help of the glass, Jonathan and his mother could see the men climbing the rope ladders and disappearing over the sides of the tall ships. They watched in silence as the British wounded were brought aboard in slings which were gently let down over the sides. Then, thunderstruck, they watched what happened next. The anchors were lifted, the sails filled, and the great fleet swung into the wind and sailed away.

"They're going." Jonathan spoke scarcely above a whisper. Then he found his voice. "We've won. We've beaten them!"

Alice Cooper didn't have the heart at that moment to tell him, but she knew the British would be back.

☆ 5

The British Return

THAT NIGHT Jonathan slept on a pallet at the foot of his mother's bed. His father did not come home, but he sent Benjamin Andrews with the word that he was all right and that they were not to worry about him. He sent special word to Jonathan, telling him to take good care of his mother.

"How many men do you think they have, Benjamin?" Alice Cooper's voice was steady.

Benjamin had lived in the woods all his life. He did not know how to give an evasive answer.

"Cap'n calc'lates there's about three thousand of 'em, ma'am."

"And how many men are at the fort?"

"Wal, I figger if the militia come in the way we

calc'late they will, there'll be about six hundred of us by mornin'."

Jonathan looked at his mother but she had turned to the table where she was wrapping some venison jerky for Benjamin.

"Well, thank you, Benjamin, for coming. Good night, and be careful."

"Yes, ma'am, thank you and good night to you both." He picked up the food pouch and started for the door. Then he stopped, turned around, and looked at them. "Mrs. Cooper, ma'am, don't worry. Colonel Mitchell is a good officer. So's your husband. They know what to do." Then he was gone.

After that, they ate their supper. Jonathan's mother got the old musket from the shed, loaded it and stood it against the wall at the head of her bed. They lay down with their clothes on. "Good night, Jonathan, try to sleep."

"I will. Mother, do you think they will try a night attack?"

"No. And even if they do, your father and the men are waiting." They were both quiet for a minute and then his mother said, "Jonathan, you are not afraid? For me, I mean."

"No, Mother, I'm not afraid. But I wish you would let me watch tonight."

"No. Every good soldier must rest, and there will be a great deal to do tomorrow."

"Well then, will you promise me something?"

"If I can."

"Promise me that if anything happens and there is something—really something I can do—you will let me go."

She didn't answer him right away. Finally she said. "All right, Jonathan, I promise."

And so they slept; neither of them very well, but better than they had expected.

The morning of the sixth of May was clear and bright. There was a steady, inshore headwind and the British were there to take advantage of it. This time a man-of-war called the "Magnet" came right up into the offing; Jonathan could read the name clearly on the hull as the great ship hove to. Ten other vessels sailed in toward the mouth of the river, while the remainder of the fleet stayed in the same position it had held the day before. Jonathan had just heard the clock on the mantel strike ten when the bombardment of the fort began.

The garrison returned the fire, but it soon became evident that they were no match for the greater British force. One by one the guns in the fort were disabled. From the front of his house, Jonathan could see the sally port at the rear of the fort. The British were not quite far enough into the river to command the same view. So they were unaware of Colonel Mitchell's next move. When it became obvious that he could not hold the fort, he sent most of his men out through the sally

port and into the brush, eastward of the stockade. He left a few men to man the remaining guns in the battery.

Jonathan tried to locate his father among the men who were filing out, but there was so much smoke he could not see clearly. The men were no sooner in position than the small boats, filled with infantry and marines, appeared again and headed straight for the brush-covered shore. Jonathan swung the glass back toward the fort once more in time to see a company of sailors scaling the bluff in a direct assault. The old twelve-pounder spoke again, mowing down the first two lines of sailors with deadly grapeshot. The infantry remaining in the fort fought bravely, but they were so badly outnumbered that within a few minutes the British had gained the top of the bluff and were swarming over the ramparts.

Jonathan could not see what was going on inside the walls, but all at once a British sailor appeared on the southwest rampart and started to take down the flag. He was halfway up the pole when he stopped, hung there for a minute, and then fell back upon the ground. A second and a third tried it, each being shot by the hidden sniper before he could get to the flag. Finally on the fourth try, the new, fifteen-star flag came down and the British flag went up in its place. Jonathan lowered the glass and passed it to his mother. There were tears in his eyes.

Alice Cooper had not wanted to take the glass away

from her son, but now she grasped it eagerly and swung it in the direction of the shore where the militia were fighting. There was a great deal of smoke, but she could see that there was a vicious battle going on. For over an hour the garrison had withstood the attack, but now as the British flag went up over the fort, she could see a change taking place. Apparently Colonel Mitchell had ordered a retreat. She could see the troops and the militia moving slowly back into the woods. They moved regularly and in good order. She felt a surging relief. James must be all right. Jonathan asked his mother for the glass.

"Father and Colonel Mitchell have called a retreat," he said. "That must mean they are going up to the Falls to protect the supplies. But the British are not following. They're going up into the fort, instead."

"They don't know that most of the supplies, the important ones anyway, are at the Falls," his mother replied. "They think they're over there at the fort or here in the village."

Jonathan's face shone with relief. "Then the great rope is safe."

"For the time being. And every one of us has to be very careful that we don't let anything slip which would let the British know where the rope and everything else really is."

Jonathan looked at his mother in astonishment. "Nobody in Oswego would tell," he said.

"Not intentionally. But sometimes things slip out."

"Well, I wouldn't—" Jonathan began but he was interrupted by the sound of running feet and Carlos Colton's breathless shout from the road.

"Jonathan! Mr. Bronson's loading stores—on the 'Syren'!—going to sink her—he needs help!" Carlos got it all out in one breath and then he dropped down on the doorstep to recover. Jonathan looked at his mother. She seemed to hesitate.

"Mother, you said if I was needed, really needed—"

"I remember, Jonathan. Of course you can go." She kept her voice even and stifled the impulse to say. "Be careful."

"I won't be long, Mother. You had better go inside and wait. I'll come right back if there is any sign of the British heading this way."

Alice Cooper stood watching the two boys until they had disappeared around the corner at the foot of the street. Then she went inside the log house and closed the door.

6 ☆

Captured!

CARLOS STARTED OFF down Aries Street with Jonathan hard on his heels. Running along behind him, with his eyes on the back of Carlos' dark head, Jonathan thought how much he admired this rangy, nervous boy who was his best friend. Carlos and Jonathan were nothing alike. Carlos was like quicksilver. He was fourteen; two years older than Jonathan. He knew how to catch a salmon in his bare hands; he could fletch an arrow as well as an Oneida; and last year, in the school spelldown, he had spelled *caoutchouc, phthisic,* and *Michilimackinac* without even pausing for breath. On top of that, he was half Spanish! He had hair and eyes almost as black as Onundiaga's and people said his mother's father had come directly from Spain. Carlos was named for him, they said.

Carlos liked Jonathan because Jonathan understood him and because Jonathan had books and liked to read. Together they had pored over the maps in the navigation books, because Carlos wanted to be a sailor and someday go to Spain. He had longed to go aboard the "Oneida" when she had been berthed in Oswego. And even now, as they ran, he kept shouting back to Jonathan things he had noticed about the British ships.

By the time they had rounded the corner, Jonathan had caught up and the two boys ran on together to the corner of Gemini and First Streets where Mr. Bronson's warehouse stood. A little group of people, mostly older men and boys, were hurriedly carrying bags, boxes, chests, all manner of things, out of the warehouse and down the wharf to the "Syren." They looked like a little army, all dressed in their sheep's-gray uniforms.

Jonathan and Carlos ran into the building, picked up the first things that came to hand, and started running for the ship. Jonathan discovered that he had a chest of tea; Carlos was carrying hard bread. They were about halfway to the end of the wharf when the sound of gunfire began again. Jonathan felt a hand on the back of his neck and then a hard push. He fell on top of Carlos and they both dropped their boxes which bounced off the dock into the water. Jonathan turned his head to see what had happened and found that Mr. McNair was lying face down beside him, and that it was he who had pushed him.

"Keep your heads down, both of you," Mr. McNair shouted. "There's a sniper's nest over there and they're trying to stop us." He flung his arms over both of the boys and they lay flat on the wharf, their heads buried in their arms. A few minutes passed, and then Mr. Mc-Nair got up, telling them that it was safe now. Jonathan looked across the river; he could still see puffs of black smoke and hear the musket fire. But now there was firing from another direction; apparently not all of the militia had retreated after all. Jonathan ran back to the warehouse for another box, wondering if his father could possibly be involved in the skirmish.

They worked as long as they could and then Mr. Bronson came up from below the wharf and said that the British were crossing the river. He conferred for a moment with Mr. McNair, and then Mr. McNair, his red hair waving like a flag in the sunlight, hurried off down the street and disappeared into his own ware-house. Then Mr. Bronson ordered everybody back near the warehouse. After that, he went down to the "Syren" himself and pulled the last of her sea cocks. By the time the gig bearing the British officers came abreast of the wharf, only the coping of the gunwales could be seen above the water.

Jonathan's attention had been divided between the sinking ship and the approach of the British gig. But now he felt the blood begin to pound in his ears; he was face to face with the enemy!

Two seamen jumped out and tied the gig to the dock. Then the men who had been sitting in the stern stepped out. Jonathan knew they were officers, but he wasn't prepared for the whisper which rippled among the men standing behind him.

"It's Yeo and Drummond themselves!" one of them said.

"How do you know?" another replied. "You've never seen them."

"No, but I've seen those epaulets before," the first man answered. "I didn't spend ten years in the old navy for nothing."

Everyone quieted as the two officers walked down the dock until they stood just in front of the warehouse. Carlos nudged Jonathan and whispered, "They look just like everybody else."

"Of course they do. What did you expect them to look like?"

"Well, you remember that time we were talking to Jed Davis and he said that the British were all eight feet tall!"

"Yes, and somebody else said they had horns and a tail. You didn't believe that too, did you?" He supposed it was Carlos' Spanish imagination coming out, but still Jonathan was frankly surprised.

"No." Carlos' tone was defensive. "No. But I did think they'd look different."

"Well, they do, in a way," Jonathan said. "Just look at those uniforms."

The boys and everybody else were dazzled by the brilliance of the British naval uniforms. They were a deep royal blue and it seemed to Jonathan that they were covered with gold lace. The hats were black, wide-brimmed with a great sweeping white plume. And both men wore smooth white silk stockings and gleaming black shoes. Their sword hilts sparkled in the sunlight and they walked as if they owned the earth. If they intended to impress the Americans by appearing in full-dress uniforms, they had succeeded; if they sought to frighten them, they had not. The taller of the two men swept the little group with a cold and calculating glance.

"Now see here." His voice sounded like steel striking an anvil. "This is Sir James Yeo, commander of His Majesty's fleet on Lake Ontario. I am George Gordon Lord Drummond. If you will look around you will see that we will brook no nonsense. Your fort, if that is what you are pleased to call it, is in flames."

Jonathan swung around and looked across the river. Great plumes of smoke and flame were leaping from the barracks his father and the other men had worked so hard to build. Jonathan felt a hard knot begin to tighten in his stomach. Lord Drummond's icy voice was continuing, "All available stores are being loaded into our ships." He stopped and looked directly at Mr. Bronson. "It is a pity you have gone to so much trouble sinking these two ships. They will be raised at once and taken back to Kingston with the fleet. Orders have been given that no personal harm is to be done any of the villagers; unless of course, you provoke it. Now you, sir"—he pointed at Mr. Bronson—"you appear to be the man in charge here. I want you to furnish pilots to take these boats over the bar."

"I beg leave to inform you, sir, that all the men capable of doing what you ask have left the village. I have no pilots to offer you." Mr. Bronson's tone was courteous but there was an edge in his voice.

Lord Drummond's face turned dark red, and with two quick strides he seized Mr. Bronson by the collar and flung him back against the wall of the warehouse.

"Then go yourself, you dirty little colonial, and take the boat out. And if you get her aground, blast you, I'll shoot you!"

Jonathan and Carlos stood as if chained to the spot. They had never heard anybody talk that way before, and neither of them could imagine anybody doing it to Mr. Bronson. There was a deadly silence on the wharf while everybody waited to see what Mr. Bronson would do.

Without a word, he stepped away from the wall, settled the front of his coat, and started toward the first boat. In the meantime one of Lord Drummond's junior officers had been standing by, listening to the villagers whisper among themselves. Now he stepped over to the Commander and said, "That man is the public store-keeper, sir; he may be useful to us."

Sir James Yeo stepped forward then, and spoke for the first time.

"Is what my lieutenant says correct? You are the public storekeeper here?"

"Yes, sir," Mr. Bronson replied.

"And you are my prisoner?"

"That, sir, is self-evident." Mr. Bronson's tone was still civil.

"Well then, sir, I want you to tell me all about the public stores; what has been sent to Sackets Harbor and Niagara, if any; what has been detained at posts in the rear; and what, if any, is concealed in the vicinity. If you will give me full and correct information on these points, you can remain here; if not, you will be taken a prisoner to Quebec." Again silence covered the wharf.

"Well, Sir James," replied Mr. Bronson, "my books and papers have been sent away for safety; I do not think I could give you this information if I would, and I am sure it would be inconsistent with my duty for me to do so if I could."

"I have nothing to do with your duty," the Commander snapped. "All I have to say is, if you give the information I want correctly you can stay; if not you go to Quebec."

"Very well, sir." Mr. Bronson's voice was still

steady. "That settles it. I will go to Quebec but I will not go willingly." And with that Mr. Bronson walked over to his little office and sat down in his rocking chair. Jonathan had once heard someone ask Mr. Bronson why he kept a Boston rocker in his office. Mr. Bronson had said it was where he liked to sit while he was making up his mind. Sir James was furious.

"Take that man aboard the 'Prince Regent,'" he shouted to his flag captain, "and take care of him!" With that, Sir James spun around and, followed by Lord Drummond, stepped into his waiting gig. The sailors slid into their places and began to pull at the heavy oars, slowly turning the boat down river in the direction of the fleet.

The flag officer stood watching the boat work its way into the main current of the river. Then he pulled himself stiffly erect and, beckoning to two seamen, went over to the door of the office. There they stopped, uncertain what to do next. Finally, the officer turned and looked back down river after the slowly retreating gig. Sir James saw him, and standing up between the oarsmen he shouted, "Take him!" So not knowing what else to do, the two seamen picked Mr. Bronson up, chair and all, and started toward the waiting gig. Jonathan watched, not believing what he saw. Mr. Bronson sat there just as if he were sitting on his own front porch.

The men who had helped to load the "Syren" were

still standing helplessly next to the warehouse. Some of them had worked for Mr. Bronson for years, and Jonathan could guess how they felt. Then all at once a strange thing happened; somebody began to laugh. In an instant the laughter spread through the little group until everybody was hooting and shouting together.

Jonathan's face flamed. He shouted to Carlos, "Why are they laughing? They musn't laugh at Mr. Bronson!"

Carlos stood for a moment without answering, his face red and working. Then he said, "They're not laughing at Mr. Bronson. Look at the British. They're laughing at the British!"

"That's right, Carlos." The boys felt a hand on their shoulders. They looked up to see Mr. McNair standing behind them, his weskit hanging open and his hair standing on end. "They're laughing at the British. Look there, boys, will you look at those sailors carrying Alvin? Did you ever see anything funnier than that?"

Mr. McNair was right. It did look funny. The British sailors were wearing long white trousers with wide bottoms which flared out, so that they looked like bells. They had on short blue jackets and wide-brimmed, flat black hats. But they had their hair tied back in little pigtails and the pigtails were coated with tar. Jonathan supposed that was to keep them in place. Now, because they were bent over under the weight of Mr. Bronson and his chair, the little pigtails stuck straight up in the air and the jackets stuck out behind.

Jonathan poked Carlos in the side and pointed. "They look like turtles," he gasped, "like bow-legged turtles." He started to laugh; he couldn't help it. Carlos laughed then, too, and Mr. McNair shouted, "Turtles," and laughed louder and harder than ever. The sailors' faces got red and their pigtails quivered but they had to keep going. Finally they got to the gig. They bent down and put the chair forward in the boat, Mr. Bronson still sitting firmly in it. Then the sailors got in behind him and started rowing out toward the "Prince Regent." Jonathan could tell that they were saying something but he was too far away to hear what it was.

By now the laughter had just about spent itself. Mr. McNair took out a big blue handkerchief and wiped his eyes. Then he put his hands back on the boys' shoulders and gave them a little squeeze.

"There's a lesson in this for you, lads. Alvin Bronson has dignity and he is a quiet man. But he used a weapon against these bullies that's more powerful than their guns. He made them look foolish. A good laugh in the right place has won many a battle. Now you remember that, do you hear?"

"Yes, sir," Carlos and Jonathan answered together. They weren't sure they understood, but if Mr. McNair said that their laughter had helped Mr. Bronson, then it must be so.

"Well now, boys"—Mr. McNair was stuffing the

handkerchief back inside the pocket in the tail of his coat—"those officers are beginning to look interested in me. I think I can be of more use to Alvin and everybody else if I get down river and join the militia. You get on home now and let your mothers know you're all right." And with a wave of his hand he headed off down First Street. The boys stood quietly, looking after him. Jonathan thought that with his red hair and long flapping coattails, he looked a little like one of the great crested herons that nested in the reeds by the river. They watched until Mr. McNair had disappeared around the corner of Taurus Street, and then they turned and ran down to the end of the wharf.

The gig carrying Mr. Bronson was just drawing alongside the flagship and there was a conversation between the men in the gig and those on the ship. Finally, a sling was lowered and Mr. Bronson, still sitting in his chair, was lifted out of the gig and up over the side of the "Prince Regent," where he passed out of sight. That made it all seem so final. The two boys looked at each other and then started back up the wharf toward the warehouse. They walked along in silence for a few minutes. Finally Jonathan said, "Do you think Mr. McNair's right? About the laughter winning battles, I mean?"

Carlos walked along, kicking a stone with the toe of his shoe.

"I don't know, but look"—he pointed at a squad of

sailors just coming around from behind the warehouse —"they do look like turtles." And Carlos started to laugh again. Jonathan looked at him and then before he could stop himself, he started to laugh too. The two of them stood there on Mr. Bronson's wharf and laughed until the tears came into their eyes.

"What are you two laughing at?"

The boys stopped as if someone had struck them. The voice was like the north wind—high and thin and just as cold. They looked up into the hardest pair of eyes they had ever seen. A marine corporal was standing there, blocking the way. He had his hands on his hips and his feet planted wide apart. The sailors came to a halt behind him.

"So you think this is funny, do you?" His voice cut into them like a whiplash. "Well, we'll see. You!" He stabbed a finger at Carlos. "You worked for Bronson, didn't you?"

"What if I did?" Carlos answered, steadying his voice as best he could.

"Well, Bronson has just told us where the stores are hidden and you may as well do so too, and save yourself a trip to Quebec."

Jonathan caught his breath; it all depended on Carlos now. The safety of the great rope and everything else depended on his answer.

"I don't believe a word of it!" Carlos' voice was loud and clear and he looked the corporal straight in the eye.

Jonathan looked at Carlos. He was speechless with relief and admiration. He never really thought his friend
would tell, but still, you had to be very brave to face up
to these men the way Carlos did. Several of the sailors
laughed, but the corporal was not amused.

"All right, then, you just come along with us. We'll
see if you don't sing a different tune when we get you
on board the 'Magnet.' Who's this?" He appeared to
notice Jonathan for the first time.

"He's a friend of mine, that's all," Carlos replied.

"Did you work for Bronson too?" The corporal's
sharp eyes seemed to bore right through Jonathan.

Jonathan, determined to stand with Carlos, said,
"No, but I helped to load and sink the 'Syren' before
you got here."

"You're a plucky one, too, aren't you?" The corporal's lips twitched but he did not smile. "Well, we
don't want you. Now get along home, you're under
foot here." The guard moved up and surrounded Carlos. Then they started off down the wharf. Carlos
turned and called back, "Stop and tell my mother what
happened."

Jonathan nodded and waved. He stood watching the
guard taking Carlos away. This could not be happening. This was May 6, 1814, and his best friend was
being captured and taken away aboard an enemy ship.
Things like this just didn't happen.

Carlos, still surrounded by the guard, climbed into a

longboat and it pulled away from the wharf and started down the harbor. Suddenly it seemed to Jonathan that Carlos looked very small sitting there among all those sailors. But his head was high and he never looked back. Jonathan watched until the longboat reached the "Magnet" and pulled around into the lee side, out of sight. Then he started walking slowly back toward First Street. How could he tell Mrs. Colton? What would he say?

He was still trying to frame the words in his mind when he got to the corner of First and Taurus Streets. A woman's voice was crying, "Stop that, leave that alone!" He looked up Taurus Street toward the sound.

A squad of soldiers and sailors was moving down the street, taking things out of the houses. The woman was still shouting and holding onto a soldier's sleeve, beating at him and trying to make him drop a pewter pitcher he had just taken out of her house. The soldier was paying no attention to her; he didn't even try to push her away. He just kept walking on down the street.

Jonathan stared in horror and disbelief. Then he felt a sharp pang and the blood started to hammer in his ears. His mother was alone! In the excitement he had forgotten all about her. Jonathan started down First Street as fast as he could go. His heart pounding in his throat almost choked him. What if he wasn't in time? What if the British got to the top of Aries Street first?

☆ 7

The
British Are
at
the Door

ALICE COOPER stood in the doorway watching her son as he came running up the hill. She had seen what had happened on the wharf through the glass, but had lost sight of Jonathan behind the buildings. For a moment she felt her knees go weak as he came, breathless, into the dooryard.

"The British are coming! They're taking things!"

"Sit down and catch your breath. I saw them. But it is not likely they will come up this far." She went into the house and brought him a dipper of cold water. Jonathan thought nothing had ever tasted so good. His mother stood by while he finished drinking. She bent to take the dipper from him, and it was then that she saw the two soldiers. They had cut in between the houses instead of coming up the road.

"Go into the house, Jonathan," she said quickly. The change in her tone made him start; then he saw the soldiers.

"But Mother—"

"Don't argue with me. Do as I say!" Jonathan went inside, with his mother right behind him. Jonathan thought she was going to bar the door, but instead she walked over and hung the dipper on its peg. Then she opened a drawer in the hutch cupboard and took something from it. Jonathan couldn't see what it was because she dropped her hand into the folds of her skirt; then she turned and walked back to the door. The soldiers were just coming into the yard.

"Good afternoon, ma'am." The man's voice was pleasant, even courteous, but his eyes were like flint.

"What do you want here?" Jonathan had never heard his mother's voice so cold.

"Well now, if you'll just step aside, ma'am, we'll take a look around." The second one didn't say anything, but his eyes were looking over her shoulder into the house. Jonathan thought, I wonder if he can see Great-grandmother Cooper's silver pitcher on the hutch?

"I will not step aside." Alice Cooper's voice was low and even but there was something in it which made both men stop. "If looking around is what you want to do, I have something to show you." And she brought

her hand up from the folds of her dress. In it there was a gun. Jonathan had never seen it before. It was small, the smallest gun he had ever seen. The sunlight glinted on the barrel which seemed to be made of silver. Jonathan could hear the dull hum of a bee hovering over a patch of clover beside the door.

"It is small, but it is deadly," Alice Cooper said.

The men looked steadily at her and she looked straight back at them. Then, suddenly, the first soldier took off his tall leather hat and bowing low, swept it to the ground at her feet.

"The Americans have won at least one battle today," he said. And with that, the two men turned and walked quickly away down Aries Street. When Jonathan could speak again, he said, "Mother, where did you get that gun?"

"It's a long story, Jonathan. Someday when we have time I'll tell you about it. Come in now and we'll have supper." She made her voice sound calm. She was grateful for the long skirt; he could not see how her legs were shaking.

They didn't talk much while they were having their supper. After what she had done, Jonathan felt shy and strange with his mother. He wanted to tell her how proud he was, but he couldn't find the words. He found himself thinking about the story he had read in the newspaper Onundiaga had brought from Salt Point. The story had told about Mrs. Dolly Madison, the

President's wife, and how when the British captured Washington and burned the President's House, Mrs. Madison had run right into the burning building and saved the Declaration of Independence and George Washington's picture. Jonathan thought, at the time, that she must be the bravest woman alive. Now he thought it would be a fine thing if Mrs. Madison could meet his mother.

As soon as it was dark, Alice Cooper opened one of the shutters a little way and pulled the high stool over in front of it. She told Jonathan to make up his pallet on the floor again tonight and then she sat down on the stool, the little gun cradled in her lap.

"Aren't you coming to bed, Mother?"

"In a little while, Jonathan. I want to make sure we don't have any more visitors."

"I'll watch with you," he said and rolled out his blankets.

"Only one of us can see through the shutter at a time. You rest for a few minutes and then I'll call you."

"All right. But if you see anything, call right away and I'll come and help."

Jonathan stretched out on the soft straw and began to go over all that had happened during the day. And then he remembered. Mrs. Colton! He hadn't told her about Carlos. He jumped up and started for the door.

"Jonathan! Where are you going?"

"I have to see Mrs. Colton. I forgot to tell her about Carlos!"

His mother looked into Jonathan's tired, distracted face. He was carrying so many burdens on his twelve-year-old shoulders. "Oh, Jonathan," her voice was near to tears, "I am so sorry. In all the excitement I forgot to tell *you*. Mrs. Colton was up here today, watching with me. She saw everything through the glass. Now go back and lie down."

Relief washed over Jonathan like a warm spring rain. "How is she?" he asked.

"At first she was very upset. I had all I could do to keep her from going down there. But then Mr. McNair came by on his way up river. He told her he was sure the British wouldn't harm Carlos. And then he said she was not to worry. You musn't either."

"All right, Mother. I'll try not to." He went back and lay down on his pallet again. He still didn't feel quite right about it. It was a simple thing Carlos had asked him to do and he had forgotten.

He turned his head toward the window; Carlos was gone. He was prisoner of the British. Jonathan kept repeating it to himself but still he couldn't make it seem real. There was something else, too. He was very worried and upset about Carlos, but at the same time he couldn't help wondering what it was like on the British ship. He didn't want to admit it, even to himself, but Jonathan was a little bit jealous of Carlos. He was in danger, of course, but Mr. McNair had said the British probably wouldn't hurt him and in the meantime he was sailing on a great ship of the line, all the way to Quebec! Jonathan had never been any farther away than his grandfather's farm which was only six miles east of Oswego. He lay there trying to imagine what a trip in a great ship like the "Magnet" would be like.

Jonathan heard his mother call. He jumped up and ran to the window. It was broad daylight. He had been asleep.

"Look, Jonathan." His mother was pointing toward the harbor. They were leaving; the British were leaving! The great fleet under full sail was moving majestically down the harbor and out into the lake.

"Father will be coming home!" Jonathan realized that he was shouting. His mother didn't mind. "Yes, very soon, I think." Nothing in her voice betrayed what she was thinking. They had had no word. She did not know if James was safe. But Jonathan had no doubts. At that moment he had no doubts about anything; the British were leaving.

His father did not come home right away, after all. He sent Ben Williams again, with word that he was all right. But he would have to stay up river until they decided what to do about the supplies.

The time passed very slowly for Jonathan and his mother. Nearly three weeks later, on the evening of

May twenty-seventh, James Cooper came home. Onundiaga was with him. Jonathan was chopping wood
by the front door when he saw them coming up the
hill. He dropped his axe and started running.

"Mother, Father's home!"

When she stepped into the yard to meet him, James
could see the trace of tears still clinging to the corners
of her eyes. Jonathan had never seen his father look so
tired and so dirty. His boots were mud up to the knees,
his handsome uniform coat was ringed with sweat
stains, and he had the dirtiest face Jonathan had ever
seen.

Jonathan ran over and threw his arms around his father, hugging him as hard as he could. Ordinarily he
wouldn't have dreamed of doing such a thing, but just
now it seemed exactly the right thing to do. James
Cooper thought so too; he bent over, and cradling Jonathan in his free arm, pressed his cheek against the
boy's hair. Neither of them said anything.

Then Jonathan turned and walked over to Onundiaga. His tall Iroquois friend was leaning against a tree
watching the scene unfolding before him. Jonathan was
struck again with the thought that Onundiaga never
seemed to look out of place; he blended in and became
part of the trees, the hills, and the river. Even now he
appeared completely at ease. He stepped away from his
tree, and placing his long rifle against a corner of the
house, he slipped a long bow and a quiver of arrows

from his shoulder and placed them carefully on the ground. The bow was made from the wood of the beech tree and it had been polished until it gleamed like aged molasses.

Jonathan had once asked Onundiaga why the Indians still used bows and arrows, now that they had guns. Onundiaga had said that the bow was quiet and that the arrow could whistle out of the forest and leave no sound, no smoke, no flame. The enemy would turn and see only the unbroken line of the trees. Jonathan cleared his throat and then he said, "Did—did you get to use your bow this time, Onundiaga?"

The steady black eyes look straight at him and nodded. Jonathan felt a shiver of pride run through him; it was a fine thing to have Onundiaga for a friend! He turned to ask his father if he had seen Onundiaga using the bow and arrows, but a glance at his parents made him decide his question could wait. His mother was putting her hands on his father's face and saying, "Oh, James, your face!" And then she started to laugh or cry, Jonathan didn't know which.

"It's the black powder," his father said, with a tired grin. "You know black powder leaves a smudge on your face every time you fire a rifle or a musket."

"Yes, but we've only seen you after you've been hunting. Now you look as if you were wearing a mask."

Jonathan thought his mother had said it very well.

That's just how his father looked; as if he were wearing one of the Iroquois devil masks Onundiaga had shown him. His mother still had her hands on either side of his father's face. Now she pulled his head down and kissed him. "I don't care how you look," she said, "just as long as you're home." When she stepped back they all laughed, even Onundiaga. She had a black streak from the tip of her nose to the end of her chin.

After supper they all went outside and sat under the trees for a while. Then James Cooper wrote a dispatch and gave it to Onundiaga with the instruction that he was to carry it to Colonel Mitchell at the Falls.

"This business will be over soon, Onundiaga, and then you can go back to being the best mail carrier in the north country. In the meantime you make a very fine military courier." Onundiaga nodded. He rarely talked, but Jonathan could tell he was pleased. The tall Indian got to his feet, gave them the Onondaga sign for farewell, and started off.

Jonathan looked at his father thoughtfully. "Do you really think the war will be over soon, Father?"

"Yes, Jonathan, I do."

"But what about the great rope and Commodore Chauncey?"

"We have a plan. That's what's in the dispatch I gave Onundiaga. We've spent the last three weeks at the Falls taking the supplies over the waterfall in flat-bottomed scows. Now they're stored on this side, waiting for me to come back up river with enough boats to get them to Sackets Harbor. I have just sent word to Colonel Mitchell that there are enough boats here and that they have not been damaged. The great rope and all the other things are going to the Commodore right away."

"Right away? You mean tonight?"

"No, not tonight. But I leave again for the Falls the first thing in the morning. Then we will load the stores into the boats and start immediately for Sackets."

"But James"—his mother's tone was serious—"that's sixty miles. And the British are out there just waiting for you to try something like this."

"It's a chance we have to take, Alice. But I don't think they'll be looking for small boats, and anyway not so soon."

"Father," Jonathan's heart was in his voice, "do you think I could go with you? I can row as well as anybody, better than most."

"I know you can, son, but what about your mother?"

"Mother isn't afraid. I just told you how she drove the British away from the house."

His father's voice was very gentle. "But that was an emergency. Would we willingly leave her alone if one of us could be with her?"

Jonathan felt his face growing hot with shame and embarrassment. He hadn't thought of it that way. "I— I'm sorry, Mother. I didn't think."

His mother touched his hand. "I know how you feel, Jonathan, but remember how you helped with the 'Syren'? There are so few men left in the village. You can't tell when you might be needed again." Jonathan looked sharply at his mother. She had said that he was a man; but just the same he couldn't help wishing he was fifteen and sure that she meant it.

Where
Is
Boat
Nineteen?

THE NEXT MORNING was gray and misty. There was a chance of a south wind and rain by afternoon. Jonathan and his mother went down to the slips with his father. The British had not bothered to destroy the Durham boats or the big open bateaux. There were ten Durhams and nineteen bateaux. Jonathan's father had decided not to take the Durhams. They were all right on the river and only three men were needed to pole them, but they would be tricky to navigate on the lake and he didn't have the skilled boatmen he needed.

The bateaux would do the job nicely, he thought. They had been the best small craft on the frontier for two hundred years. They were wide and almost flat-bottomed. With five men on a side to do the rowing, he was certain he could get all the stores, even Jonathan's great rope, into them and safely up the lake to Sackets.

Jonathan and his mother stood near Bronson's wharf watching his father begin to organize the men who were going to take the boats up river to the Falls. He divided them into crews of ten each with five to a side. Suddenly he turned and looked back to where Jonathan and his mother were standing. He said something to the men who were with him and then started back up the wharf. He walked straight up to Jonathan's mother and said bluntly, "Alice, I need Jonathan."

"What for, James?" Her face had gone white but she kept her voice even.

"I didn't know our casualties had been so heavy. We lost sixty-nine men. Some of them were my best oarsmen. Jonathan knows how to row as well as a man. I need him to help us get the boats to the Falls."

"And will you take him all the way to Sackets?"

"I can't answer that until we come back through here on our way out."

She did not hesitate, not even for a minute. "All right, James." She walked over to Jonathan and put both of her hands on his shoulders. Then she bent and kissed him gently on the cheek. She hadn't done that for a long time. Her soft fichu brushed his cheek and Jonathan caught the scent of lavender. All of a sudden he thought of the loft at night when he was little.

He cleared his throat and said, "You needn't worry, Mother. I will be careful." Somehow he didn't want her to have to say it this time.

"You will need something to eat. I'll go back and get it while you are getting the boats ready." The level of her voice told Jonathan that she understood. She hurried off down First Street while Jonathan, still unable to believe his good luck, helped his father and the other men check the caulking and the oars. As they were moving into position to start, his mother returned with his father's biggest hunting pouch, full nearly to bursting.

His father laughed when he saw it and teased her gently. "The Falls are only six miles up and six miles back, Alice. You've got enough food there for a trip to Salt Point."

His mother's voice was steady but she did not smile. "Or a trip to Sackets?" she said.

His father had been standing on the gunwale of a boat. Now he stepped down, took the pouch in one hand and her hand in the other. "Thank you, Alice," he said and kissed her cheek. Then he and Jonathan climbed into the boat and pushed off. Jonathan waved to his mother and then bent to his oar. These boats were heavy, much heavier than the little skiffs he was used to; but rowing was something he knew how to do, no matter how big the boat was.

They maneuvered quickly into a long line; Jona-

than's boat was number fourteen and he was the third oar on the port side. He put his back into it and pulled with all his might. It was hard work. The Oswego River was white water and rapids almost all the way to the Falls, so it took them nearly two hours to make the trip. Finally, as the boats ahead of him rounded the bend at Bundy's Point, Jonathan could see the quiet water below the Falls. He was glad the end was in sight; he had begun to feel the strain through his neck and shoulder muscles. It was a good thing the boats were empty, as long as this part of the journey had been against the current, he thought.

There was nothing to see at the Falls but the ruins of Colonel Bradstreet's little fort left over from the old French War, and the temporary shelters where the stores were hidden. The shelters were made of leaves and branches and they looked like part of the forest, until you got right up to them.

When they hove to and began to pull for the shore, Colonel Mitchell and the troops appeared out of the forest and lined up along the bank waiting for them. They sent up a rousing cheer when they saw the little flotilla, and some of the men splashed out into the water, caught hold of the prows, and pulled the boats halfway up onto the shore.

The loading started immediately. First came the heavy armament: there were twenty-two long thirty-two-pound cannons, ten twenty-four-pounders, and three forty-two-pound carronades. Next came the eight cables for the "Superior's" mainsail, and finally the great cable itself. Jonathan couldn't really believe a rope could be that big, not even when he saw it. It was going to take one boat all by itself to hold the great rope. The men pulled it in a coil from its hiding place to the edge of a little bluff just above the shore. They paused when they got there and looked to James Cooper for directions as to which boat was to receive it. Jonathan's father hesitated and then, with a smile, pointed to boat number fourteen. It was Jonathan's boat!

Joyfully Jonathan ran over and hopped back into his boat with the rest of the crew, while they backed the bateau under the bluff. Then they all got out and held the boat by the gunwales, steadying it as the men above began letting the great rope slip over the edge of the bluff and down into boat fourteen. Down it came, slowly, slowly, like a big yellow-brown snake, coiling itself in a great heap in the bottom, the boat sinking lower in the water. For one awful moment Jonathan thought the cable was going to be too heavy for the bateau and they would not be able to carry it. But, at last, the great brass-bound end came over the bluff and down with a final soft plop.

The boat was steady; the great rope could begin its journey. Jonathan and the crew got in very slowly and carefully. They settled themselves tightly between the great rope and the side of the boat. Then the other stores were loaded into the remaining boats and the oarsmen took their places. After that the riflemen came aboard; one hundred and thirty of them under Major Daniel Appleby. They waited, all lined up along the shore for the signal to move down river. Then Jonathan's father stepped up on a large rock and spoke to the waiting flotilla.

"We will go directly to Sackets Harbor. There will be no stopover in Oswego, since it will be near sunset when we get there and we want to get out on the lake and into the shadow of the shore line as soon as we can. A body of one hundred and thirty Oneida warriors will meet us at the mouth of the Salmon River, which is about halfway to Sackets. I do not have to tell you that speed is the most important thing we have to consider right now. Colonel Mitchell will remain here awaiting further orders. Captain Woolsey of the United States Navy will assume command until we reach Sackets Harbor."

As one man, the oarsmen lifted their oars and held them upright and dripping in the clear afternoon sun. Jonathan held his the highest of all; it was official now. He was going all the way to Sackets Harbor with the great rope!

The mist had lifted and now the day was as bright and promising as their adventure. Jonathan's father dropped his hand and the boats put out into the down-stream current. Soon they were stroking and whirling their way through the rapids and the white water down river to Oswego. Jonathan couldn't contain himself. He pressed his leg against the great rope and began to sing:

> It oft times has been told,
> That the British seamen bold,
> Could flog the tars of France
> so neat and handy—o.

His voice grew stronger as they went along. Soon the other men took up the refrain. They didn't know the words, so they hummed and Jonathan sang, all the way to Oswego.

His mother was standing on the wharf when they arrived at the village. The boats slowed as they passed the wharfs, but they did not stop. Everybody who was left in the village was lined up on the jetty.

Jonathan dropped his oar for a moment and raised both arms over his head in a salute to his mother. Then as the assembled villagers shouted, "Godspeed!" the flotilla swept out into the harbor. They glided past the three little Indian fishing islands at the mouth of the river, and then pulled in toward the eastern shore of Lake Ontario.

The boats kept in a line about ten yards out from the shore line. They rowed for almost two hours in the soft summer twilight, talking and singing; some of the men smoked their short clay pipes filled with sweet Virginia tobacco. Then, as darkness closed in over them, word drifted back through the boats, "Pipes out; talk over." Jonathan turned to the man behind him. "Why can't we talk? We'd hear the British before they could hear us, wouldn't we?"

"Can't tell, son. Sound carries a long way over water. Hush now."

The hours crept by as they went on; there would be no moon tonight and now it was black dark. No sound broke the stillness of the night save the rhythmic dip and sweep of the oars. Then a new command was whispered back through the boats. "Raise oars and listen." Each time they heard it the crews obeyed, and each time the silence was broken only by the call of the night birds and the heavy breathing of the men. Finally the man in front of him turned to Jonathan and whispered, "We're nearing the Salmon River."

Jonathan swung around in his seat to relay the word. As he did so, he felt something wet brush against his face. It felt almost like a hand. In an instant he knew what it was. Fog! The heavy summer fog that brought dread with it into the heart of every north country boatman. Soon Jonathan could not see the man sitting in front of him. It was as if thick layers of uncombed wool had been laid over the boats. He reached out from time to time and touched the rope, just to make sure it was still there.

The oarsmen slowed their pace to one stroke a count

and inched along through the quiet black water. Jonathan's heart hammered in his throat. Suppose they got lost! Suppose they missed the mouth of the river and drifted out on the lake instead! Then he felt the bottom of the boat hit something. Rushes! They were in shallow water. The word came back; they had reached the mouth of the Salmon River.

The faithful Oneidas were waiting and helped to beach the boats. Jonathan looked shyly at the hard brown bodies of the Indians, gleaming in the early dawn light. They wore no shirts and their faces were painted—red, yellow, and white. They had tomahawks and pistols in their belts and great silver rings swung in their ears. They looked fierce and frightening, and Jonathan was glad they were on his side.

He moved toward the prow of the boat and when no one was looking, reached out and gently patted the great rope. Then he stepped up on the gunwale and slowly and painfully let himself down over the side. When his feet touched the sandy shore, he almost fell. He had never been so tired in his life and his feet were numb.

His father's hand caught his elbow and steadied him. "Just a minute, Jonathan, until I check the boats. Then we will find a place to rest." Jonathan nodded, and stamping his feet to get the circulation going again, he slowly followed his father to the center of the line.

James Cooper began the count. "Fifteen?" "Here, sir." "Sixteen?" "Here, sir." "Seventeen?" "Here, sir." "Eighteen?" "Here, sir." "Nineteen?" There was no answer. "Nineteen?" his father said again. Only the lapping of the waves and the lonely hoot of a loon answered him.

Suddenly Jonathan felt a gust of cold wind slap against his face; it sent a chill all the way through him. He forgot about being tired. Where was the missing boat? Was it lost, had it foundered or—Jonathan shook his head but the thought would not go away—had the British found boat nineteen? He followed his father to the end of the line where Captain Woolsey was waiting.

"Boat nineteen is missing, sir," his father said.

"It's this confounded fog." Captain Woolsey's voice was rough with fatigue and frustration. "It would have been a miracle if we had gotten through with all of them. Now the British know what we are up to."

"Can you be certain, sir?" James Cooper tried to sound optimistic. "Maybe the boat just got separated from us and has found its way to shore by now. McAllister was in command of nineteen and he's a good man."

"I know he's a good man but he can't work magic," Captain Woolsey said. "Yeo's probably got them, Jim, and figured out what we're trying to do."

Jonathan's father's voice was steady as he answered. "But if we can get to the mouth of the Big Sandy, we have a chance."

"You know, I think you're right." Captain Woolsey's voice was thoughtful. "Get me the best Indian runner we have."

Jonathan's father went over and spoke to the Chief of the Oneidas. Within minutes a tall Indian appeared out of the mist. It was Onundiaga. But a different Onundiaga from the one Jonathan knew. Now he was wearing war paint and he had a steel hatchet and two handsome, silver-mounted pistols in his belt. Jonathan pulled at his father's sleeve.

"Onundiaga's here and he's painted for war, but he isn't an Oneida. He's Onondaga."

"Jonathan," his father replied, "you are forgetting that Oneida and Onondaga are both Iroquois."

Captain Woolsey gave Onundiaga an urgent message to Commodore Chauncey at Sackets Harbor explaining what the situation was, and requesting reinforcements to meet them at the mouth of the Big Sandy as fast as they could. As soon as Onundiaga had disappeared into the forest, the men squatted on the ground, Indian fashion, and ate a cold breakfast of dried jerky and hard bread. The meal was finished in less than ten minutes and then the boats put out again.

They were all exhausted, but there was no time for rest now. They crept along the shore, hardly daring to breathe. The fog had lifted and the sun was coming up, hot and searing. The lake lay open and clear; there was no place to hide. The boats scraped along in the shallow inshore water, sliding under overhanging trees and rocks wherever they could. Finally, at noon, they reached the shelter of Big Sandy Creek. They went on a mile or more up the south branch of the stream and then beached their boats. Stiff and sore, Jonathan climbed from his seat and stumbled toward his father.

"How far are we from Sackets Harbor?" He was so thirsty, his voice was only a whisper.

"Only about twenty miles." James Cooper opened his canteen and gave the boy a sip of water.

"Do you think the reinforcements will get here before the British find us?" Jonathan asked and then took the water, holding it in his mouth for a moment before swallowing, as Onundiaga had taught him to do.

"We can't be sure about that," his father answered, "but isn't Onundiaga the best runner we know? I think we can count on him."

And James Cooper was right. They had barely made camp by midafternoon when out of the woods came a company of cavalry and one of artillery, straight from Sackets Harbor. Onundiaga was riding back-saddle on one of the first horses, his gorget and hatchet glistening in the sun. He looked very pleased with himself. They had scarcely had time to congratulate him when a company of infantry came marching through the brush to make Onundiaga's victory complete. Captain Woolsey came over and started to speak to Onundiaga. Just then a sentry came running in from the lake shore. There were two British gunboats, three cutters, and a gig closing in around the mouth of the Big Sandy.

"So we were right. Yeo did find McAllister and boat nineteen." Captain Woolsey's voice was clear and firm. "And they mean to close with us here. Well, let them. I think we may have a surprise or two in store for Sir James Yeo and His Majesty's most excellent navy. Now, make camp, have a cold supper, and get to sleep early. I will want all of you at battle stations one hour before first light."

Jonathan walked over and helped with the bed rolls and the stacking of the oars. Then, just before it was time to bed down for the night, he slipped down to the shore and took one last look at his boat. The great rope was still coiled like a powerful, sleeping snake. Jonathan looked around. A trout arched high out of the Big Sandy and then fell back with a wriggling smack; two dragonflies touched down on the great rope for an instant and then darted away; a sentry surveyed the horizon and then turned slowly and paced back. Everything seemed safe and under control. Tomorrow would be a new day, for them and for the British. Jonathan walked quietly back to the camp circle and lay down for the night.

☆ 9

The Great Rope

IT WAS STILL DARK when Jonathan felt a hand on his shoulder. As he lifted his head, he could see a soldier moving soundlessly among the sleeping men, touching each one lightly as he passed. The Indians rose together, like wisps of smoke, and stood motionless, waiting.

"What time is it?" Jonathan whispered to his father.

"About an hour before first light. Come, we must hear Captain Woolsey's plan. But be very quiet."

Silently Jonathan got to his feet and followed his father. Captain Woolsey was standing near the center of the line of boats and he delivered his orders quietly and quickly. The troops from Sackets Harbor were to be stationed behind the line of boats which was just above the bend in the stream. Jonathan was glad to know that trained regulars would be protecting the great rope. A little below the bend, the riflemen and the Indians were hidden in the thickets which lined the banks of the creek. James Cooper joined the riflemen and ordered Jonathan to take cover well back in the woods behind the lines.

"Please, Father," Jonathan had to speak out. "I can load for you and I promise to keep well down and out of sight."

"I'd let him do it, Jim." It was Captain Woolsey who spoke as he passed down the line. "We can use rapid fire this morning."

Jonathan's father hesitated a moment, and then he agreed. It occurred to him that if he could use his pistol while the rifle was being loaded, it might make all the difference.

James Cooper had chosen a fallen tree for his cover. It was at least two feet thick and clustered tightly with tiny branches. It was the expert rifleman's perfect line of defense. They lay there quietly for almost an hour; it reminded Jonathan of the times his father had taken him deer stalking. In fact, he thought, it's practically the same thing. The black flies were thicker than it seemed they ought to be for May. He rubbed a little mud on the back of his neck to protect it. Then, just as the rim of the sun appeared over the edge of Lake Ontario, the British ships appeared, moving slowly up the creek. They waited until they were in sight of the

American boats and then they began a sharp and vicious cannonade.

Jonathan felt a pang of fear in the pit of his stomach. If they hit his boat, the great rope might sink to the bottom of the Big Sandy. He lifted his head very slightly and peered over the rim of the tree in the direction of the boats. The British had forgotten one thing; the boats were so heavily loaded that they sat low in the water. The cannon fire was passing harmlessly far above them. Seeing that this was getting them nowhere, the enemy landed a flanking party on either bank of the creek and moved slowly forward, pouring grapeshot and canister into the bushes. With a loud cry, most of the Indians on either side of Jonathan rose as one man and fled into the woods. Jonathan was astounded. He could not imagine anyone running away from a just cause like this one. Then he felt a soft thud at his side; turning, he found Onundiaga stretched on his stomach beside him.

"Oneida!" Onundiaga said and spat into the grass.

Jonathan felt better. He knew Onundiaga would never run away from a fight. He lifted himself up to tell Onundiaga what he thought, but the Indian's hard brown hand shot out and forced his head down into the soft marsh grass. The British fire whistled over their heads, showering leaves and branches down upon them like summer rain.

Jonathan's father turned his head and said, "Just a

few more minutes and then we'll show them." As he spoke, the British ships and the flanking troops came into range at the same time. Jonathan's father rose to his feet and shrieked like a Huron. At once all the other rifle and militia men rose and poured a withering fire into the surprised English troops. It was a perfect ambush. Jonathan lifted his head while he reloaded his father's rifle. Just at that moment, the American artillery opened fire. The British boats were raked fore and aft by small arms and cannonade. There was so much smoke and so much noise that for a few minutes Jonathan couldn't tell what was happening. And then it was all over. Out of the smoke and confusion appeared a British officer with a small white cloth tied to a bayonet. The British were surrendering. The whole battle had lasted just a little more than ten minutes.

Onundiaga unfolded his long body and stood up. *"British!"* he said. *"Oneida!"* He spat again and walked away into the drifting smoke. Jonathan got to his feet and stood beside his father. Then he watched the British force surrender to Captain Woolsey.

As soon as the white flag had been accepted, all firing ceased and the smoke slowly cleared away. The British moved as if they had rehearsed what was to come next. They tied their boats, which had been badly damaged, alongside the bateaux. Then their sergeants marshaled the soldiers and sailors together, one hundred and seventy of them in all, and lined them up along the shore.

They looked as if they were going on parade—the regulars buttoning their red tunics and straightening their shakos; the sailors adjusting their blue jackets and pulling their flat black hats forward on their heads. Jonathan smiled again when he saw the pigtails. He looked for the two men who had come up to the log house, but they were not with the surrendering troops.

After that, Captain Woolsey gave an order and all the American units—regulars, militia, and the Indians who had remained—lined up facing the British. Jonathan had never seen anything like it before in all his life. The entire British raiding force was surrendering. Their ranking officer, who was an army major, stepped forward and saluted Captain Woolsey. Then he drew his sword, and first turning its hilt over his arm, he presented it to the American commander.

"Would you care to review my men, sir?" he asked.

Captain Woolsey politely declined. "That will not be necessary."

The Major saluted again. "Then, sir, I surrender this force to you in the name of His Most Sovereign Majesty George III, by the grace of God, King of England, Scotland, Ireland, and the Isles.

Colonel Woolsey returned the salute and the Major's sword. Then he addressed the men, telling them that they would be detained here awaiting further orders. The Major dismissed his men, who were then broken up into small groups and taken to a bivouac area where an American corporal's guard was assigned to watch them. The wounded, who had been treated where they fell, were taken down the road to a little farmhouse which had been converted into a field hospital.

Jonathan waited while all this was going on, to see if there was anything his father or Captain Woolsey wanted him to do. When he could see that nothing more was going to happen right away, he went up to his father and said, "Father, may I go down to the boat and see if the great rope is all right?"

"Yes, and Jonathan, make sure the boat is still tied."

Jonathan hadn't thought of that. Maybe a stray bullet had cut the tether and his boat with the great rope was drifting free. He ran as fast as he could, but when he got to the beach, all the boats were safe and the great rope was just as he had left it. While he was walking back toward the camp, he thought about all that had happened since daybreak that morning. There had been a battle and a final surrender, and the whole thing hadn't taken two hours. The problem facing them now was how to get the great rope and the other supplies to Sackets Harbor.

Captain Woolsey, Jonathan's father, and the other officers met in conference shortly before noon. His father took Jonathan along and he sat quietly on the ground, at his father's feet, listening.

"We don't dare risk the lake again," Captain Woolsey was saying. "Yeo is waiting out there for his fleet to return and when it doesn't, he'll be patrolling every inch of the coast between here and Sackets."

"Maybe we could chance it by night?" one of the junior officers said.

"They'd be down on us at the first squeak of an oar-lock. No, we've got to think of something else." There was a pause. Then Jonathan's father spoke with his usual quiet deliberation.

"We could take them overland." The men all turned and looked at him.

"Overland!" one of them said. His tone was almost scornful.

"Overland," Captain Woolsey repeated, thought-fully. "Overland! By George, I think we can at that! The road isn't very good, but we have enough men and if we go out and cover the farms, we'll have enough wagons. If we all go at it, I think we can do it!" He walked to the center of the camp and called for the ser-geants to assemble the troops. The men came at the double and stood in a circle around him.

"Men, we can't take the supplies to Sackets by water. But if you are willing, I think we can take them overland. I want a detail of fifty men to spread out through the countryside and borrow every farm cart and wagon you can find. Try to be back by nightfall. Time is the only thing we can't spare."

The detail was formed within minutes but it seemed to Jonathan an eternity before they came back.

During the afternoon, the men who had remained in camp had been busy building shears to aid in unloading the heavy freight and lifting it onto the wagons. Jonathan had been amazed at how quickly the men cut down the trees and shaped them into timbers which were erected into frameworks for the unloading mechanism. The way in which the timbers were crossed and lashed together to support the block and tackle for unloading looked like a pair of scissors. Jonathan wondered if that was why they were called "shears." He decided to ask his father about it sometime when everybody wasn't so busy.

About sundown the wagon detail began to return to the camp. They had every kind of vehicle to be found on the frontier. There were two-wheeled oxcarts, heavy farm wagons, and even a closed carriage. The wagons were pulled down and drawn up near the boats at the water's edge.

After the carts were assembled and the shears erected, Captain Woolsey called a halt for the night. Jonathan was disappointed; he had thought they might work right on through, since there was so little time. His father assured him that the work would begin first thing in the morning, but that now the men were tired and would work better and faster if they were rested.

Jonathan was the first one up and ready to go the next day. At first light the unloading began, and Jonathan's impatience grew when he realized how slow the work was going to be. He had thought they would be all finished and ready to go by afternoon. But very soon he saw that even if the men worked as hard and as fast as they could, it would still be several days before the job would be finished.

Finally, on Thursday morning, the second of June, the unloading of the boats and the reloading of the carts were finished; everything was snugly packed away— everything except the contents of boat fourteen. There wasn't a cart or wagon big enough to hold the great rope.

Captain Woolsey stood with his hands on his hips surveying it. "What are we going to do with this cable? We've got to get it up there. Without it Chauncey can't move an inch out of that harbor."

Jonathan couldn't contain himself any longer. "We could carry it!" he shouted.

"Carry it!" Captain Woolsey repeated.

"Why not?" There was excitement in James Cooper's voice. Some of the men standing nearby had heard what Jonathan said. Now they repeated, *"Carry it! We'll carry it!"* Other voices took it up until the words spread like a chant over the whole company.

"We'll carry it! We'll carry the great rope to Sackets!"

Then Captain Woolsey called for volunteers. It seemed to Jonathan as if every man there, including the Indians, stepped forward. Jonathan stepped forward, too. Captain Woolsey looked down the long lines of men. Then he started walking along in front of them. "You," he said. "And you—and you." On down the lines he came, choosing men as he passed. Nearer and nearer he came; Jonathan held his breath. Then Captain Woolsey was standing in front of him. He paused a minute and smiled. Then he said, "I'm sorry, Jonathan, but we need the broadest backs and strongest arms we have for this job."

"Yes, sir," Jonathan said but he swallowed hard.

"However," Captain Woolsey went on, "we need a water boy. These men are going to get very thirsty." Jonathan brightened at once.

"Yes, sir!"

After he had calculated the weight and length of the great rope, Captain Woolsey chose two hundred men to carry it. They hurried down to the shore and began pulling it out of the boat until it stretched four hundred feet down the military road. Then the men all lined up beside it.

Jonathan's father stepped into his place at the head of the line. He looked back along the length of the rope and then he shouted, "Pick it up, men!" All together, the men bent and lifted the great rope to their shoulders. James Cooper lifted his head and shouted, "Forward, ho!" And the strange caravan was off. It was only then that Jonathan noticed that Captain Woolsey had chosen militia men to carry the great rope. The rest of the men picked up wagon tongues or put their shoulders to the wheels and fell behind. A small detachment of regulars was assigned to accompany the column. The remaining regular troops stayed with the prisoners at the Big Sandy.

Jonathan filled a large goatskin water bag from a cask on one of the wagons. Then he ran along the road until he was about even with the middle of the column. He swung in beside a big militia man from Bundy's Point. The man grinned at him. "Start up a song, lad."

Jonathan was about to comply when one of the regulars who was walking beside him said, "Not yet, we're still too near the lake. Wait until the road bends inland." So Jonathan and his friend from Bundy's Point grinned at each other and swung on down the road. In a few minutes they came to a place where the road straightened out and Jonathan could see down the length of the entire column. The great rope was as big around as a young tree and stretched out on the men's shoulders you could scarcely see the end of it. If you walked on the rope side of the column, you couldn't see the men's heads. Jonathan thought it looked like some gigantic animal walking along on hundreds of legs.

"It's so long and strange looking," he said, not realizing he was speaking out loud.

"Aye, lad." His friend from Bundy's Point had heard. "Not since Hannibal crossed the Alps has there been a stranger military column than this."

(CANADA)

ONTARIO

ST. LAWRENCE

HORSE ISLAND

SACKETT'S HARBOR
SMITHVILLE
ELLIS VILLAGE
BIG SANDY CREEK
SALMON RIVER

OSWEGO · FORT ONTARIO

OSWEGO FALLS

OSWEGO R.

LAKE ONEIDA

NEW YORK STATE

LAKE CAYUGA

LAKE SENECA

···· ROUTE OF THE GREAT ROPE

After a while the road took a sharp turn to the right. They began to move inland. Soon they were some distance from the lake. The forest grew thicker on either side of the road and the mosquitoes and black flies began to plague the marchers. The trees cut off the lake breeze and the men began to sweat. Finally they stopped for a short rest; Jonathan ran from one man to the next giving them drinks from the waterskin. They rested less than ten minutes and then took up the march again. Since they were now a safe distance from the lake, Jonathan began to sing. He chose the tune he had been told was the favorite marching song of the armies of 1812.

> *Hey, Betty Martin, heel and toe,*
> *heel and toe,*
> *Hey, Betty Martin, all tip toe.*

The men joined in for a few minutes, but then their voices trailed off and finally stopped altogether. It was too hot and the road was so deeply rutted and hard to walk on they needed all their strength just to keep going. Then Jonathan noticed that the great rope had begun to gall the shoulders of some of the men. He ran to one of the supply carts and made pads from some of the blankets. Then he ran along beside the men and slipped the pads under the rope where it touched their shoulders. While he was making the pads, Jonathan noticed that some of the men's shoulders had begun to bleed; but nobody mentioned it, nobody complained. The only sounds breaking the silent afternoon were the tread of the marchers, the creak of the wagons, and the steady drone of the flies and mosquitoes.

Suddenly, one of the regulars came bursting out of the forest. A British raiding party had been sighted about a mile to the north. That meant that the British were ahead of them. The men carrying the great rope put it down, and then dropped on their stomachs on top of it. The wagons were pushed into the brush and the regulars fanned out along the road ahead.

It was very quiet. Jonathan could hear all the sounds of early summer; a gull screamed overhead, and a crow answered him. An orange butterfly circled and wheeled and came to rest on one of the men's backs. He caught the sharp scent of wild mustard and the clean smell of new grass. He thought how strange it was that he should be noticing all these things when the British might be down on them at any moment. Then, as quickly as it had happened, it was all over. The British had gone on toward the lake. They hadn't seen the column.

The march continued until they got about halfway between Ellis Village and Smithville. There Jonathan's father called a halt and they made camp for the night. A double watch was appointed and no cook fires were permitted. Jonathan didn't mind the cold food or the mosquito bites or the damp, hard ground. He curled up with his arm over the great rope and slept as if he were back home, tucked under the eaves in the loft.

The night passed quietly. At first light, everyone ate some jerky and hard bread, and then the men got to their feet and the march resumed. By ten o'clock the heat and the insects had begun to be bothersome again, and Jonathan was busy once more running up and down the line with the waterskin. Finally, a little past noon, he got to the head of the column where his father was walking. Just as he got there, the man marching behind his father stepped in a hole and fell. The column jerked to a halt and Jonathan's father let down his section of the rope. He bent to look at the man's leg. He had broken his ankle. James Cooper called to one of the regulars, who picked up the injured militiaman and took him to one of the carts. After that he turned back and bent to pick up the rope again. Jonathan saw his chance.

"Father, let me take that man's place. I'm as tall as he was. I know I can do it. Please, Father."

James Cooper looked into the eager, anxious face of his son. He had never seen such longing. It was only a little farther to Sackets.

"All right, Jonathan, pick it up. Forward, ho!"

Jonathan stepped into the line and picked up the great rope. At last he was doing it! He was helping to carry the great rope! He had to sing!

Hey, Betty Martin, heel and toe,
heel and toe.

Now it was his song, too.

Very near the end of that long and eventful day, just
as the sun was beginning to redden and slip beneath the
rim of the lake, the road broke into a clearing. There
were a few houses, the blockhouse of a fort, and be-
yond, a perfect blue crescent. It was Sackets Harbor.
They had made it. They were there. But best of all, the
great rope was there; the great rope was in Sackets
Harbor.

Nobody gave an order, but suddenly the men all
pulled themselves erect. They began to march as if
they were on parade and everybody started to sing.
This time, it was "Hail Columbia, Happy Land." People began running out of the houses then; they lined
the road and started to cheer. One of the men who had
been acting as a scout ran up ahead and unfurled the
company flag. Down through the center of the little
village the column marched, straight to the harbor
shore.

There it was, the "Superior." It was the biggest ship
Jonathan had ever seen. It mounted sixty-six guns and
could carry a full man-of-war crew. Standing on the
deck at attention were Commodore Chauncey and his
entire staff. And standing right beside them were Car-

los and Mr. Bronson! Jonathan couldn't believe his eyes. He stumbled and nearly dropped the great rope. Never taking his eyes off Carlos, Jonathan marched with the column down to the water's edge where they laid the great rope in the protecting curve of Sackets Harbor. Carlos had seen him and was starting to wave. Wildly, with both arms high over his head, Jonathan waved back.

"Father, Father," he shouted. "It's Carlos and Mr. Bronson! How did they get here?"

His father, waving too, and equally surprised, answered, "I don't know, but they're coming ashore.

We'll find out in a few minutes."

A gig from the "Superior" started down the harbor, with Commodore Chauncey, Carlos, and Mr. Bronson sitting in the stern. As soon as it had touched the shore and its passengers had stepped out, Captain Woolsey advanced to meet them, saluted smartly, and said, "Captain Melancthon T. Woolsey reporting, sir. The stores you requested are safely transported. We regret the loss of one boat. However, we have replenished her stores with equipment captured in the battle. I have no information about her crew."

Commodore Chauncey returned the salute and then

turned to the company. "I salute you and your men, sir, and am happy to tell you that information received when Mr. Bronson and Carlos were released gives us to understand that your missing boat was captured and the crew is safe. The northern frontier and the entire United States of America are forever in your debt."

Then everybody was cheering. People were gathering around the great rope to look at it. Mothers were bringing their children to touch it.

As soon as Commodore Chauncey stopped speaking, Jonathan and Carlos raced toward each other. At first they couldn't say or do anything but pound each other on the back. Finally Jonathan gasped, "How are you? What did they do to you? Did you go to Quebec? How did you get here?"

"Whoa, Jonathan." His father had just come up. "One question at a time."

Carlos paused for a minute and Jonathan thought he looked just a little disappointed. "I'm fine. We didn't go to Quebec—only as far as Kingston. They didn't do anything to me. The sailors were fine. Drummond and Yeo are almost as mean to them as they were to Mr. Bronson. The sailors don't like them any better than we do."

"But how did you get here?"

"They only kept us in Kingston a few days and then they sailed over here to blockade Commodore Chauncey. They let me go right away. Then Commodore

Chauncey sent word to Lord Drummond that Mr. Bronson didn't have any military secrets and that he was really a civilian, so they let him go, too."

"Then did they go back to Kingston?"

"No, they're still out there. You can't see them, they're over behind Horse Island. But they're right there watching to see that Commodore Chauncey doesn't try to get out of the harbor."

"That's all going to change now." The boys whirled around and found Commodore Chauncey standing behind them. "Thanks to these militiamen and their commander here, we have our supplies and our armament. We can fit out the 'Superior' now, and then I think Sir James Yeo will look at things quite differently." He smiled at Jonathan. "And who is this?"

Jonathan's father saluted and then introduced Jonathan, explaining how he happened to be along, and how it had been his idea to carry the great rope.

"It was the best idea anybody on the northern frontier has had since the war started," the Commodore said. "You can't take a frigate out without an anchor. Young man, since you have helped to take such good care of her main cable, I think you should have a remembrance from the 'Superior.'" He beckoned to a seaman who was standing nearby. .

"This is Tom Watson," the Commodore continued. "He's the bosun on the 'Superior' and he can carve bet-

ter than anybody I have ever seen. He carved that
bosun's whistle you see hanging around his neck, and if
I remember, it has a picture of the 'Superior' on it.
Tom, don't you think your whistle would make a fine
present for the young man who brought us the great
rope?"

"Yes, sir. Begging your pardon, sir, but if you'll wait
just one minute . . ." Tom Watson reached in his
pocket and took out his seaman's knife. Then he took
the whistle and with the point of the knife began doing
something to the side of it. In a few minutes he was finished. He winked at Jonathan, saluted, and gave him
the whistle. It was the finest whistle Jonathan had ever
seen. It was made of whalebone, smoothed and polished
to a soft golden color. On one side was a carving of the
"Superior" and on the other was the picture the bosun
had just done—a length of the great rope and the in-
scription, "Jonathan Cooper, June 4, 1814."

Jonathan was so surprised and pleased he couldn't
think of anything to say except, "Thank you." The
bosun and the Commodore seemed to think that was
quite enough. They said good-bye and then started
back for the "Superior." Jonathan wrapped the whistle
carefully in his handkerchief and then looked up to
find Carlos looking at him with a very strange expres-
sion on his face.

"Did you do all those things?" he said.

"What things?"

"All that your father was telling the Commodore about carrying the rope and everything."

"Oh, well, a man hurt his foot and I just took his place, that's all."

Carlos looked at Jonathan as if he were seeing him for the first time. "Could I have a look at your whistle?" was all he said.

IO ☆

Home Again

AND SO THE ADVENTURE WAS OVER. They had done the impossible. They had fooled the whole British naval force on Lake Ontario and they had gotten the great rope to Sackets Harbor.

It was three days before the Oswego men could start for home. They needed the rest, and besides, since they had to go back overland, they wanted to make sure there were no British raiding parties waiting for them. The scouts came back on the morning of the third day and said that the way was clear. So, with all the "Superior's" flags flying and the cheers of the villagers ringing in their ears, the company formed ranks and started for home. They were going to return the borrowed farm carts when they got back to the Big Sandy, and so Jonathan, Carlos, and Mr. Bronson got to ride part of the way on a big harvest wagon. Mr. Bronson particularly needed space in the wagon—for his rocking chair.

The journey back over the military road to Oswego took them five days. A scout ran on ahead to tell the villagers they were coming. When they got to the forks in the road, just before the turnoff to Fort Ontario, they saw the whole town waiting. Most of the women and children had returned by this time, and they were all there.

But in that crowd Jonathan saw only his mother. She was standing a little apart from the rest. She had on her good blue dress with the white fichu and her best linen apron. Jonathan stepped out of line and ran faster than he had ever run before; faster even than the day he ran to tell her the British were coming. She met him halfway and right there in the middle of the military road, he hugged and kissed his mother as hard as he could. His father was right behind him and soon they were all mixed up together, laughing and crying and not caring who saw them. It didn't matter anyway, everybody else was doing the same thing. Carlos' father had picked him up, right off his feet, in a great bear hug. And little Mrs. Bronson kept saying again and again, "Alvin, they gave you back your chair!"

When they finally got home, Jonathan was certain there was never any place as beautiful as the big square room in the log house at the top of Aries Street. His mother began right away to set things out for supper.

He could see she wanted to talk to his father, so Jonathan went out to the shed and got the shovel. Then he ran to the corner of the house and dug beneath the chokecherry tree. His books were still there, wrapped in the canvas, dry and safe. He took them in and put them on the table beside his plate while he ate his supper. His father looked at his mother and his smile was warmer than the candle's glow. "I'm glad to see that your books are safe, Jonathan," was all he said.

Next morning, when Jonathan woke up, the sun was high in the gable window. He rolled out of bed and hurried over to look out. It was midmorning. He had never slept so late in all his life. He dressed as fast as he could and slid down the ladder. His father was long gone and his mother was just setting the churn on the step outside the door. The steeple clock on the mantel said half past ten! His mother's eyes were merry and bright when she looked at him. "Did you rest well, Jonathan?" she said.

Jonathan could feel himself blushing. "Yes, but why didn't you call me? It's almost noon."

She laughed then and said, "Not quite. Anyway I think you missed a good deal of sleep over the past weeks. This just helps you to even the score."

She always put things so well. She had a way of making everything come out right, he thought.

His mother came across the room, ruffling his hair as she passed. "There's something here for you. Onundiaga brought it last night, just before he left for Salt Point." She handed him a bundle wrapped in a piece of hide and tied with a rawhide thong. The minute he touched it, he knew! His hands were shaking so, he could scarcely untie the lashings. His mother came over and helped him with the last knot and together they opened Onundiaga's gift. Out rolled a pair of beaded moccasins and a buckskin shirt trimmed with yellow porcupine quills. It was very quiet in the room for a few minutes and then his mother said, "Why don't you go up and change your clothes, Jonathan?"

That night, as Jonathan lay in his bed tucked snugly under the eaves, he put out his hand and touched his shelf. Everything was still there, including the new things he had put there today. It was black dark now in the loft, but he could feel them all. There was a one-pound round shot, half a goose egg, three books, a buckskin shirt trimmed with yellow porcupine quills, and a whistle.

He picked up the whistle and tucked it under his pillow. Then he slid his hand in under his head so that one finger just touched the whistle. Even in the dark he could feel it—its shape, its smoothness, and the carving on its sides. His finger traced over the lines: "Jonathan Cooper, June 4, 1814." And he knew that whenever he touched it, he would see again the long line of marching men, walking down a rutted road on a June after-

noon; that he would smell again the sharp, musky odor of new-woven hemp; and that he would feel again, nestled against his cheek and lying firm across his shoulder, the rough, hard, wonderful burden of the great rope.